STORM CHASERS

A Novel

PAUL QUARRINGTON

St. Martin's Press ❧ New York

Text Design: Kelly Hill

www.stmartins.com

Library of Congress Cataloging-in-Publication Data

Quarrington, Paul.
   [Galveston]
   Storm chasers : a novel / Paul Quarrington.—1st U.S. ed.
      p. cm.
   ISBN 0-312-34281-0
   EAN 978-0-312-34281-4
   1. Islands—Fiction. 2. Hurricanes—Fiction. 3. Caribbean Area—
Fiction. I. Title.

PR9199.3.Q34G35 2005
813'.54—dc22   2004061913

First published in Canada under the title *Galveston* by Random House Canada

First U.S. Edition: July 2005

10 9 8 7 6 5 4 3 2 1

STORM CHASERS

After Four a-clock the Thunder and Rain abated, and then we saw a *Corpus Sant* at the Main-top-mast Head, on the very Top of the Truck of the Spindle. This sight rejoiced our Men exceedingly; for the height of the Storm is commonly over when the *Corpus Sant* is seen aloft; but when they are seen lying on the Deck, it is generally accounted a bad Sign.

A *Corpus Sant* is a certain small glittering Light; when it appears as this did, on the very Top of the Main-mast or at a Yard-arm, it is like a Star; but when it appears on the Deck, it resembles a great Glow-worm. The Spaniards have another Name for it (though I take even this to be a *Spanish* or *Portuguese* Name, and a Corruption only of *Corpus Sanctum*) and I have been told that when they see them, they presently go to Prayers, and bless themselves for the happy Sight. I have heard some ignorant Seamen discoursing how they have seen them creep, or, as they say, travel about in the Scuppers, telling many dismal Stories that hapned at such times . . .

—WILLIAM DAMPIER, *A New Voyage Round the World*

THERE ONCE WAS AN ISLAND named Dampier Cay. It lay to the southwest of Jamaica, making a triangle with that country and the Caymans. Dampier Cay was, technically, under English governance; it retained the pound as its official currency, for example, even though no one on the island accepted, or carried, the local money. All transactions were made using the American dollar.

Dampier Cay was a narrow strip of land, a few miles long, that nature had pushed forth from the water for no good reason. Still, it was land, and people built there. Because there was not much of it, property was relatively expensive. Some wealthy white people owned estates. The black people who worked for the white people lived in a tiny hamlet,

Williamsville, which was near the centre of the island. Dampier Cay ran north and south, but it was bent in the middle. There was a harbour there; aside from a couple of local fishing trawlers, it was rarely used.

On either end of Dampier Cay were resorts. At the south end was a big hotel. It claimed the best beaches and was popular, by island standards, with tourists. At the north end was a place called the Water's Edge, a collection of buildings that sat near the bottom of the island's only significant hill.

That hill was called Lester's Hump. Reporters were confused by that, for a while, because after the storm a man named Lester was found at the top, along with two white women. But Lester's Hump had been so called for over two hundred years, ever since William Dampier had directed Lester Cooper to cart liquor and victuals up to the top. Dampier had seen weather coming.

> *But the Day ensuing, which was the 4th Day of July, about Four a-Clock in the Afternoon, the Wind came to the N.E. and freshned upon us, and the Sky looked very black in that quarter, and the black Clouds began to rise apace and moved towards us; having hung all the Morning in the Horizon.*

The island's east coast, much of it anyway, is a rock cliff that rises a mean height of twenty-five feet. It seemed reasonable protection should the weather and the water get into cahoots, but William Dampier had seen many odd things in his journeys, and heard much odder. He'd heard about waves that stood thirty yards tall. So he directed Lester Cooper to take the flour, sugar, suet, etc., to the summit, and the other men laughed and called it Lester's Hump.

There is, today, a small cross at the summit of Lester's Hump. It is made out of wood and whitewashed, and someone attends to it, keeping the cross pristine and cultivating a small bed of flowers around its base. At the foot of Lester's Hump there are ghostly suggestions of civilization and order—scattered timbers and pieces of metal and machinery. Further south, trees have been thrown over and lie crisscrossed, like wooden matches that have been rattled in the box and then tossed onto the ground. Beyond this is where Williamsville once stood. A handful of black people still live there, in hastily built, ramshackle constructions. Oddly, there are a few estates that stand in good condition, but the owners have boarded the windows and put up optimistic *For Sale* signs. The big hotel remains, although no tourists ever go there, because Dampier Cay no longer exists.

It was a fairly easy matter for Dampier Cay to disappear, because it had never proclaimed its existence with any authority. It was not even on all maps. Many derive from the originals made by William Dampier, who was the Royal Cartographer, although he spent much of his time buccaneering with his Merry Boys. Ironically, having named the island after himself, Dampier left it off his depiction of the area. Where it should have been dotted, Dampier fashioned a large and ornate C to begin the word *Caribbee*.

To get to Dampier Cay, in the days when it still existed, either one had to know exactly what one was doing—only one tiny airline serviced the island, the airport a glorified bungalow near Miami, Florida—or else one came by chance.

Gail and Sorvig, whom you will meet, stumbled upon the island, or at least the knowledge of its existence, at a travel agency in New York City. One of them had idly picked up a small flyer from the Water's Edge. The print was crooked, rendered out of Letraset, and announced prices much cheaper than any other resort. The flyer also featured a drawing of a bonefish, sleek and fierce-looking. The drawing was made by a man named Maywell Hope, although, when you meet him, you may find that hard to credit. Hope made the flyer and took it to the post office in Williamsville, where he and the postmistress mimeographed two hundred copies. Hope and the postmistress then used her computer to select random vacation bureaus around the world, and mailed them out.

Maywell Hope made the flyer over the protestations of Polly Greenwich, his common-law wife and the owner of the Water's Edge. Polly possessed a kind of grim optimism, and was convinced that business was as good as could be expected. Polly herself had come to Dampier Cay by chance, from New Zealand. Her first husband had died from cancer, he had withered away; and when he was gone, Polly boarded an airplane, not caring where it was headed, then she bought a berth on a cruising yacht, and one day the ship anchored at Dampier Cay. While the rest of the passengers went snorkelling, Polly wandered the small island until she came upon the collection of buildings at the bottom of Lester's Hump. She had lunch in the little restaurant and, sipping her coffee afterwards, decided to purchase the place. It wasn't a life she would have designed, but at least it was a *life,* it had purpose and parameters. There was even a bonus, a lover who came with the deal, the tall sunburnt fishing guide and transport captain, Maywell Hope.

Maywell had come to Dampier Cay by the purest of chance—he was born there. So was Lester Vaughan, retained at the Water's Edge as gardener and general handyman. The two had actually been fast friends as boys, and as young men they had shared many evenings at the Royal Tavern, consuming vast quantities of rum in honour of their ancestors. Then, you know, events had taken place. Maywell Hope no longer drank; Lester claimed he'd given it up but too often would return to the bottle. Lester would disappear, sometimes for days on end, and, when he turned up again, most often could be found sleeping it off in the tiny cemetery beside the pale blue church.

There are three more people to meet. These people came neither by chance nor by design—or perhaps more accurately, by a combination of the two. What I'm getting at is that these three came because Dampier Cay was where it was, and they had reason to believe they might encounter something there, something most people take great measures to avoid.

As soon as the tropical depression was identified, the World Meteorological Organization's Western Hemisphere Hurricane Committee gave it the name *Claire.* The practice of naming storms began after the Second World War; prior to that, hurricanes were identified geographically, for example the Great Storm at Galveston.

The Great Storm at Galveston occurred in 1900. The water began to rise in the early morning of September 8. Families gathered on the beach, and children played in the surf, delighted to see Nature behave so oddly. The chief meteorologist for the city rode up and down the strand on horseback, shouting that the barometer was plummeting and the winds were rising, and insisting that everyone seek higher ground. Many ignored him; those who didn't had no higher ground to seek, Galveston being at most eight or nine feet above sea level. The storm surge that came was fifteen feet tall. By the next morning, eight thousand people were dead.

After Tropical Depression Claire was born, it began to move westward. Meteorological bureaus posted its image, as seen from heaven, a pretty white swirl with a hole in its centre. The swirl changed position, hour to hour, and these movements were monitored by many people, most of them anxious, perhaps because it was their job to be so, perhaps because they owned property that might lie in her path.

A few people were eager to know where Claire might wander for another purpose, and they appropriated her images for their own websites, which had names like *Weatherweenies.com* and *Stormwatch.com*. These were chasers, men and women eager to encounter extreme weather. Claire was born on Sunday, and by Tuesday morning she lay in the middle of the Atlantic. The chasers began to make guesses about her trajectory, guesses based on science, history and magic.

Only three guessed right.

Many were close. There were a few, for example, who journeyed to Martinique and St. Lucia, and they were slapped by wind and made sodden by rain falling in huge sheets that rippled and roared like bent sheet metal. But in the chaser's own argot, these people merely *got wet.* The merciless elements that danced around Claire's eye passed between these two islands, on their way toward Dampier Cay.

THE CUSTOMS OFFICIAL STARED at the computer screen, trying to determine if Caldwell might be a terrorist or criminal.

"Where are you going, Mr. Caldwell?"

There was a moment of silence; being addressed as "Mr." took Caldwell by surprise. Then he answered, "Galveston," and was surprised again, by his own response.

The customs official was a plump, freckled man, and out in the world, Caldwell knew, the customs official would sweat too much. He would be irritable, he would smell bad. Some customs officials sought the profession because they craved power, or because they enjoyed repelling unwanted aliens; this one wanted only the cool blue air of Toronto's Pearson International Airport.

The official said, "You visit the United States a lot."

Caldwell made no reply. It wasn't a question.

The official made it one: "Why do you visit the United States a lot?"

"Fish."

"To buy fish?"

"No, no. To catch fish. You know. To angle."

"I see."

"And the weather."

"You enjoy the climate?"

"No. The weather."

The customs official now picked up Caldwell's passport and flipped through, perplexed. The pages were scarred with the faded impressions of entry stamps from countries around the globe. The customs official grunted, indicating that he was putting two and two together, that Caldwell was up to something. "What line of work are you in?"

"I'm in no line of work."

"How's that?"

Caldwell had annoyed the customs official, he could see that, so he proffered an explanation. He smiled as he said, "I used to be a teacher. Phys. ed. and science. But I don't need to work any more. I'm rich."

The official looked at his computer screen again, as though this information about wealth should have been electronically forthcoming. He struck the keyboard hard. "How did you make your money, Mr. Caldwell?"

"I didn't make it. I won the lottery. Sixteen million dollars."

"Whoa."

"Exactly."

His wealth made people see him in a different light; they liked him better. That used to bother him. Well, that's not entirely true, Caldwell used to let it bother him, *make* it bother him, because it was the sort of thing that *should* bother a decent man—but Caldwell laid no claim to decency, and hadn't for some years.

The plump, freckled customs official became friendlier. He riffled through the passport once more, this time in obvious admiration of Caldwell's adventuring. "So where are you off to now?"

"Miami."

"Uh-huh?"

"I'm going to a little airport just outside of Miami. I'm going to catch a plane, it'll take me to Dampier Cay."

"Never heard of it."

"No. I've never heard of it either."

"Huh?"

"I mean, I hadn't ever heard of it. It's just a little island."

The customs official nodded and offered Caldwell his passport, then pulled it away before Caldwell could put his fingers on it. "Hold it, Mr. Caldwell. Didn't you tell me first that you were going to Galveston?"

"Yeah," agreed Caldwell. "I guess I'm going the long way."

Beverly was already at the little airport outside Miami.

She'd taken a bus from Orillia to Toronto, and then a train to Buffalo, New York, and from there she'd flown to Florida. It was the cheapest way to go, although she'd had to overnight in Miami, and even the small, seedy motel she'd found cost a lot more than she'd budgeted for.

The flight to Dampier Cay was scheduled for one o'clock in the afternoon. Beverly had arrived at the airport at about seven-thirty in the morning. The place was deserted, a little bungalow beside a huge barren field cut with a strip of tarmac. At one end of this runway sat a battered twin Beech outside a rusted Quonset hut.

The cabby was reluctant to leave her there alone, that's how desolate it was. But Beverly said she'd be fine. "I'll just wait. I've got my book."

Beverly had no book. After the taxi left, she sat down on the steps and folded her hands in her lap.

At nine o'clock a small car pulled up and a beautiful black man stepped out. He was dressed in a blue uniform with golden buttons and brocade. Beverly stood and had to resist the impulse to salute.

"Good morning, ma'am," said the man.

"I have a ticket for the flight to Dampier Cay," said Beverly. "At least, I have a reservation number."

The man nodded. "That flight may be delayed."

"Why?" she asked. "Because of Tropical Storm Claire?"

"No. Just because it usually always is."

"Ah."

"Don't worry about Claire. Now they're saying she's going to miss everything, probably just blow out at sea."

Beverly nodded and smiled as though relieved. But really she knew that *they* were almost always wrong.

Blowing out at sea was only one scenario; perhaps the most desirable, but by no means the most likely. Hurricanes are created moment by moment, as though fuelled by fresh time, by nowness.

Take Hazel. Caldwell said that often, in barrooms around the globe, when he'd had three drinks too many and no desire to go up to his room. He would find some other lost soul and slowly work the conversation around to hurricanes, and then he would touch on their erratic nature. He would recite the science, hoping that his companion was too drunk and heart-sick to interrupt. "No one's really sure how a hurricane becomes organized," he'd say. "They might get influenced by an upper tropospheric short-wave trough or something." And then, while his listener's eyes were still glazed over, he'd say, "The point is, hurricanes are erratic. Take Hazel."

No one had predicted that Hurricane Hazel would work her way through the Caribbean and Carolinas, up the Atlantic coast, and then, as furious as she had been at birth, kick the province of Ontario in the ass.

Caldwell was three years old in 1954, and his earliest memory was of Hurricane Hazel. Granted, not all of the memory was genuine. For instance, part of the memory was of being put to bed by his parents, the pair of them beaming happily, proud of their little toddler. That never happened, because for one thing, his parents did nothing together. Sometimes Caldwell imagined that his own making was performed in the manner of fishes, his mother leaving a small pile of gleaming eggs in the depressed centre of the mattress, his father passing over sometime later and glumly depositing his own sticky contribution. But all that aside, Caldwell knew that his father was otherwise occupied; he was, that night, busy fighting the storm.

The story of Hurricane Hazel was every bit as important to the elder Caldwell as it would become to the younger, perhaps because it was the only time in his life that Caldwell's father did anything useful. There had been rain all that week, and the rivers and creeks to the north of Toronto were already brimming. When Hazel came on Friday afternoon and filled the world with wind and water, the rivers became riotous. The storm caught everyone by surprise—the radio reports had called merely for "rain"—but by little Caldwell's bedtime flooding was certain. So while his father may have taken a few minutes to say good night to his son, it is not likely. His father was almost certainly outside, helping to pile sandbags along the banks of the normally docile Humber River.

Back then the Caldwells lived on Kingdom Street, a block away from the river, close enough that Caldwell's father feared the basement would flood and destroy his workbench and power tools. Caldwell couldn't recall his father ever actually making anything, but throughout his life the older man maintained a professionally equipped shop in the basement of whatever house they lived in.

After being placed in his little bed, Caldwell had not fallen asleep. He had immediately raised himself up onto his knees and looked through the window. He was amazed at the sight. The rain did not come *down,* it blew in all directions. It obscured the world in the same manner in which Caldwell destroyed drawings he deemed poor, with violent cross-hatching. The boy was delighted at how musical the wind was making everything. The window glass vibrated in its frame with a low, steady hum.

Caldwell must have slept, but this was not part of his memory. He knew he fell asleep, because he had checked all the newspaper reports and the official police records. Caldwell knew the sequence of events that took place a little after three a.m., the logic and causality. The Humber River grew bigger and stronger and finally threw over the footbridge, the concrete walkway that allowed people in his neighbourhood of Westmount easier access to the shops on Weston Road. The bridge was toppled, and when it fell it became a dam, turning the water aside. The river had nowhere to go but down Raymore Drive.

Kingdom Street shared backyards with the houses on Raymore Drive. Caldwell's bedroom was at the back of the house, which means that when he once again knelt on his mattress and chinned himself up by the windowsill, he was staring at the houses on Raymore. He was never sure what woke him up, but it seems likely that it was screaming. When he grew up, it occurred to him that the houses had been too far away, the wind howling too fiercely, for him to have heard anything. But the screams may have been so anguished that they somehow pierced Caldwell's ears, and he raised himself up and saw a wall of water move down the street and gather up the houses. It did this like a janitor gathering up chairs in a grade school auditorium. By the time the river was done, it had pushed seventeen houses off the face of the earth. Thirty-five people, including Caldwell's playmate Kenny Janes, were gone forever.

And Caldwell had watched them disappear.

There were plastic chairs lining the walls of a room inside the bungalow airport, and Beverly claimed one in a corner. The beautiful black man stood behind a counter and busied himself with various chores, placing and receiving telephone calls, communicating with someone using a walkie-talkie. Beverly overheard discussions of wind speed and Mercator co-ordinates.

Other passengers arrived. The first was a man in his fifties, very neat, immaculately neat. His skin reminded Beverly of the colour of coffee when she put the perfect amount of cream into the cup. He wore a blindingly clean white shirt and blue trousers with sharp creases.

This man held a little cardboard box in his hands, very lovingly and carefully. When he sat down, he did not set the box on an empty seat; he placed it in his lap and kept his fingers curved around the sides. Beverly wondered what was in the box, perhaps a small, dead thing that the immaculate man had once loved dearly.

A short while later, two young women entered the little airport. They were nearly identical, both in their twenties and wearing T-shirts and blue jeans stretched by slightly overfed bodies. They had long golden hair and fierce green eyes. One wore spectacles, the only clear distinction between them.

These women had a lot of energy, and a lot of luggage. They spent a few moments making a wall with their bags and suitcases, then they addressed the beautiful black man behind the counter.

"We're on the flight to Dampier Cay," said one, mispronouncing the name, delivering the first part as French, rendering the second as it is spelt. The airline representative did not correct this, he only said, "The flight's been delayed a little."

"Well, that's excellent," said one of the girls. "How come?"

"We're keeping an eye on the weather."

"Oh, peachy. It's that Claire thing, right? The hurricane?"

"It's not a hurricane," Beverly piped up. "The winds haven't reached seventy-two miles an hour."

The two women sat down in plastic chairs and turned to her.

"We heard about it yesterday," said one.

"We tried to change our week," said the other. "We tried to change it, but our boss said no, the fucking prick. Now we've got to go on vacation when there's gonna be a hurricane."

Beverly could empathize, because her boss wasn't the nicest fellow either. When Beverly had announced suddenly that she wanted a week off, Mr. Tovell had threatened to fire her. She made up an elaborate fiction: her great-aunt had been arrested for uttering bad cheques, her grandfather had gone down to the police station with a pistol, demanding his sister's release, and the police had leapt upon him, shattering his jaw, and now he was going to stand trial on various charges and the old man needed Beverly to translate the moans and whines he produced through the wire. She just kept piling up details until Mr. Tovell waved a hand with weary exasperation. No one else at that workplace could have got away with it, but Beverly was associated with bizarre misfortune, she seemed to have "bizarre misfortune" tattooed across her forehead, so Mr. Tovell said, "Oh, okay, go ahead, take the days off."

An elderly couple arrived, dragging little suitcases on wheels behind them. They nodded at the man behind the counter and sat down without speaking to him, obviously familiar with the routine. They linked hands and asked each other, in hushed tones, if everything was all right. Then the elderly man looked around the room, chuckled nervously and spoke to them all. "Looks like there might be a little bad weather."

"It's not a hurricane," said one of the two girls, looking to Beverly for confirmation. "Right?"

"Yes. I mean, no, it's not. Not, um, yet."

The immaculate man lifted one of his hands from the little box and held up a finger. "What will be," he said, "will be."

On the flight from Toronto to Miami, Caldwell was one of only two passengers in first class. The other sat across the aisle, an elderly woman who seemed to be going south to die. She wore a heavy coat and a fur hat much too warm for early September, and she removed neither for the flight. The upturned lapels threw her face into shadow. After she sat down, she fell into a fitful sleep, her hands wrapped around the ends of the armrests, the fingers bloodless.

Before the flight attendant drew the curtain, Caldwell looked back into economy. It was full of tall, strapping young men of about fifteen years of age, sporting the same uniform, a bright blue blazer and grey flannel shorts, plaid knee socks and heavy brogues. They were a team of some sort, an athletic team; they grinned lopsidedly, drunk with the belief that they could kick the shit out of the world. Caldwell knew that they were returning from, rather than going to, the contest; he could tell from their glowing contentment that they had won.

Halfway through the flight, he put down his magazine and stretched. Across the aisle, the elderly woman sputtered slightly, banking away from the Great Beyond. Caldwell rose, parted the curtain and walked into the economy section.

Some of the boys were eating and some were sleeping, both activities performed with noise and gusto. Many of the boys wore headphones, not the light black discs of foam supplied by the airline but brightly coloured forks of plastic that drove deep into their ears. A few read horror novels.

Caldwell looked for the coach but couldn't see an adult among the youths. For a brief moment he imagined that *he* was the coach, Mr. Caldwell, that he was their leader. He wanted to sit down among them and leaf through *Sports Illustrated* and drift off to sleep, pleased as punch with what his boys had accomplished.

He was certain his life had held such moments before, but he had trouble remembering now. He couldn't string it together, couldn't make the events sit side by side. He could summon passages from his childhood (the memory of Hurricane Hazel was always at his beck and call); and scenes from his adulthood would sometimes arrive unbidden. But he had real problems with his middle age, the last ten years, which seemed to belong in a dream, or to someone else.

For a while he had pretended to himself that this was some fault of his faculties, his actual memory, and he'd gone to doctors, some of whom were sufficiently impressed by his wealth that they designed complex therapies and prescribed magical drugs. He went along with all this—especially the drugs—until it became clear that his inability to remember his life was due to the life itself, the great hollow that lay in the middle, a black hole that sucked in all matter. When this became clear (nothing had actually become *clear,* rather it had become less indistinct), Caldwell found pastimes. He had no interest in them beyond the fact that they consumed hours. For example, he did crossword puzzles. He didn't care whether or not he completed them; he often entered words that he knew were incorrect, and sometimes crammed two, even three, letters into the same tiny square. And he tied flies, his huge fingers clamping down feathers and bits of fur onto minuscule hooks. But Caldwell never used the flies.

His friend Denton MacAuley, hoping to cheer him up, had taken Caldwell to a fly-in lodge in northern Ontario. It was indicative of Denton's relentless optimism that he thought Caldwell simply needed "cheering up." When he invited him, Denton had said, "It's been two years," a statement he obviously found as significant as Caldwell found it baffling.

Denton and Caldwell had played junior hockey together for the Barrie Blades, and their relationship retained a kind of naked bluntness. So, even though Caldwell maintained that he didn't want to go fishing, Denton said, "Fuck off." Denton was a doctor, a cosmetic surgeon who specialized in grafting new skin onto burn victims. But when speaking with Caldwell, he was still a hockey player. "*You,*" he said, poking a finger into his friend's chest, "are going fucking fishing."

They had flown into a dreary northern outpost, and travelled to a huge log cabin where men hunted pike by day and drank heavily at night. Denton had laboured terrifically hard at creating fun; he told jokes and exchanged good-natured insults with the other sports, he roused Caldwell at five in the morning and drove him out into the dawn and into a motorboat. Denton jabbered and gesticulated and even managed to raise a smile on the face of Herbert, the Cree guide, who gave the impression of never having smiled in his life. But Caldwell was unmoved, and sat in the bow, hunched over, his hands pressed together in a mockery of prayer.

On their last day at the lodge, they stopped in the middle of the lake, a lake so large that land could not be seen at the edges. Herbert stood upright and worked the tiller, positioning the boat more precisely in the middle of the emptiness, and then he threw over a little anchor, an apple juice can filled with concrete. Denton MacAuley looked baffled. "Is there a shoal or something here?"

Herbert shrugged and nodded in several directions. "It's a good spot," he declared. "Big fish."

And it had proved to be a good spot. Denton tossed in a lure and water boiled around it. He set the hook and a huge pike came out of the water, its maw opened, making a mighty, if silent, roar. "Holy shit," said Denton.

Caldwell wasn't fishing, even though Denton begged him to. "Come on, buddy. You love to fish. You used to be a fishing machine. Look at the size of this motherfucker."

Caldwell made no answer. He was looking at a huge shadow, far away where the water met the sky.

Herbert released Denton's pike, and Denton threw the lure back into the water and had another fish on almost immediately. This one was larger still, and Denton had a hard time managing it on the light tackle. The pike came to the surface and rolled there, wrapping itself in monofilament. Herbert grabbed a paddle and poked at the fish, trying to get it to roll the other way. In their preoccupation, neither of them noticed what the shadow was doing.

It was spreading out across the face of the water.

Caldwell's rod was propped up beside him in the bow, and he heard the line snap and crackle faintly. There was no wind (there was the *sound* of wind, ever so slight, but no wind) and yet the line was twitching back and forth.

Herbert stopped poking at the fish and jerked his head upwards.

The shadow fell upon them.

"Oh-oh," said Herbert.

He swung the paddle as though it were a baseball bat, straight at Caldwell. Caldwell merely bent over, so that the paddle sliced the air over his head and connected with the fishing rod beside Caldwell, snapping it in two. Herbert struck the pole with sufficient force that both halves flew out of the boat—the reel crank caught briefly in the cuff of Caldwell's jeans, and the butt was propelled upwards—and then the sky cracked open.

There occurred an instant so strange that no one who was there—not Caldwell, not Denton MacAuley, not Herbert—afterwards described it the same way. Herbert maintained that he had heard the line crackling, and looked up to see the tempest bearing down, so he'd aimed the paddle at Caldwell's rod to launch it out of the boat, knowing a lightning strike was coming. The lightning hit the rod at the apex of its flight, and the rod carried the power into the water and the water carried it away, and that was why they were all still alive. (And, Herbert also maintained, that was why the fifty-dollar tip he'd received was wholly inadequate.) Denton, a man of science, maintained that lightning had smacked the water hundreds of feet away. The strike was nowhere near the boat, or else they'd all be dead.

But Caldwell knew he'd been hit. He felt heaven's fire course through his body. And if his heart didn't stop, it was because his heart wasn't functioning in any true sense to begin with. No, when the lightning hit, Caldwell's heart *started*, and in that moment before they began their panicked flight toward shore, Caldwell stood up, flushed and clumsy, and spoke.

"Hey," he said, "did we come here to fish or to fool around?"

TEN MINUTES BEFORE the scheduled departure time, Jimmy Newton entered the little airport. Beverly recognized him at once.

Not only was Jimmy the most famous storm chaser on earth, Beverly had once accompanied him on a tour of Tornado Alley. But she was not surprised when Newton's eyes moved across her without pausing. On that tour there had been two van loads of chasers, and Beverly had been in the group led by Larry DeWitt, with whom she'd had a one-night fling. Beverly scowled at that memory, forced it out of her mind. It's not that she was ashamed of her behaviour—she had, in the past few years, done many more shameful things—but she was still stung by the bitter disappointment of the encounter.

There were camera and computer bags slung over Newton's shoulders, and as he approached the beautiful black man, Newton shrugged and dropped these things to the ground, leaving a little trail of high technology from the door to the counter. "Okay, chief," he said. "Let's fly."

"Yes, sir," said the black man. "Only there's been a delay."

"Typical," Newton muttered.

It was the first time the black man had mentioned the delay officially, and everyone in the little waiting room came to attention. "You see," said the airline representative, addressing them all, "there is an active weather system."

"There is an active weather system which is fricking hundreds of miles away," said Jimmy Newton.

"Yes, sir. But we are trying to assess the potential danger to our passengers and pilot."

"I'll assess it for you: zilch-o."

"There is a thought that we should cancel today's flight. We'll reschedule for tomorrow. The airline would put everyone up in Miami for the night."

"Does this mean it's a hurricane now?" asked one of the young women.

"Yes," said the black man. "It's been upgraded. The weather office has issued a hurricane watch for the area, including Dampier Cay."

"Let's review the terminology," said Jimmy Newton derisively. "*Hurricane watch* means that hurricane conditions are possible within twenty-four to thirty-six hours. And the flight we're talking about only takes an hour and a half."

"I don't understand why you'd want to fly knowing that there is the potential for danger."

"Because there's not all that much potential. And even if the storm was here, it wouldn't be all that dangerous. You can fly through all sorts of systems. Hey, I flew into Floyd with the Hurricane Hunters. Right through the wall and into the eye. And Floyd was a *four*."

The man behind the counter took a step backwards and raised his voice. "Flight number 764 is delayed until further notice."

"But not cancelled?" asked Beverly.

"The matter is still under consideration." He picked up his

walkie-talkie and a cellphone and disappeared through a door behind him.

Jimmy Newton scowled, turned away, took a few steps into the middle of the room. He had a large trunk, short legs and arms, and was dressed like a little boy, Beverly noted: running shoes, white shorts and a T-shirt that he tucked into the elastic waistband. Newton put his hands into his pockets but had to hoist up the shorts first in order to do so.

"That was goddam amazing, flying into Floyd," he said to no one in particular. "We hit the wall, right, it's like we're a BB in a boxcar, you know, rattling around, and then, *whoosh* . . . into the eye. And in there it's like heaven or something, you know. It's all calm, and there's these little puffy clouds and this weird silver rain. It was like light, right, like it was raining light."

The elderly couple stood up and started rolling their little suitcases toward the door. "Where are you going?" Newton demanded.

"They're going to cancel the flight," the husband said resignedly.

"They're not going to cancel any goddam flight. Sit down."

The elderly couple obeyed. Jimmy Newton didn't sit down himself, however. He remained standing in the middle of the room, staring at something he alone could see.

Half an hour later, Caldwell opened the door to the waiting room and stepped through. He had a sailor's duffel bag slung across his shoulder, and wore dark sunglasses, which he didn't remove. Caldwell nodded at Newton, said his name quietly. "Jimmy."

"Hey, it's the fisherman."

"So," asked Caldwell, "what's going on?"

"The airline's getting cold feet."

Caldwell nodded, taking in the information. It registered on Beverly that, had the flight left on schedule, this man would have missed it. It was possible that he'd anticipated there would be a delay; he seemed a well-travelled sort, to judge from the wear and tear on his duffel bag, his deep tan. But there was another possibility, and Beverly studied the man closely to see if there was anything in his appearance that would support it. He was tall and broad-shouldered, and wore a white golf shirt and lightweight grey trousers like a phys. ed. teacher. This man was so recognizably a phys. ed. teacher, in fact, that he seemed to have been ripped from another place, another time, and set down in the strange little bungalow airport in Florida.

The beautiful black man re-entered the waiting area and came to attention behind his little counter. "I have an update on the flight 764 to Dampier Cay. In light of the warning issued by the—"

Jimmy Newton cut him off. "An airplane ticket is like a contract," he pointed out. "A legally binding contract. You people have contracted to supply a service—"

"But in cases of, what do you call it, *force majeure*—"

"Please don't cancel the flight," said the phys. ed. teacher. "I have to get over to the island. My family's there."

"Your family," repeated the black man, not as a question. He looked at Caldwell for a moment, and it was clear he understood that families should be together, especially in catastrophe. "I'll talk to the pilot." He picked up the walkie-talkie and depressed a button on its side. "Ed?" he said quietly.

Caldwell took Newton by the elbow and led him away. "So," asked Caldwell softly, "what have you heard?"

"She's just a little mewler, a newborn babe," said Newton.

Caldwell nodded, listened to the black man speak into the walkie-talkie, pleading on his behalf. "But the man's *family* is over there . . ."

"But hey," said Jimmy Newton, "there's another depression moving right behind her. I think maybe she's going to suck it up, she'll be two, maybe three by the time she hits any land. Maybe even . . ." He pressed his lips together, fearful of invoking some sort of jinx by speaking his hope aloud.

"Where are you staying?" asked Caldwell.

"Some place called the Water's Edge."

Caldwell nodded. "Me, too." Neither seemed particularly happy about it.

"All right," announced the man from the airline, stepping out from behind the counter. "Let's everybody get on the plane," he said gravely, "before the shit starts to fly."

They started across the field toward the airplane, in an order that corresponded with their arrival at the bungalow airport. Beverly was in the lead but deliberately slowed her pace, so that they all walked past her: the immaculate man, the two young women, the elderly couple, Jimmy Newton, and the beautiful black man, pulling an oversized child's wagon piled high with their collective luggage.

The phys. ed. teacher drew up beside her, and Beverly gave him a look and a quick smile. "You don't have any family on the island," she said.

"How would you know that?" Caldwell asked.

"Because I've done what you just did."

THE AIRPLANE had five rows, with pairs of seats on either side of a narrow aisle. Beverly selected the window of the middle row. She was hoping that the phys. ed. teacher would sit beside her, but before that could happen the immaculate man leapt into the seat, still cradling the cardboard box in his hands.

The phys. ed. teacher was the last to mount the stairs into the belly of the Beech. He scanned the available spots and claimed the nearest window seat. Jimmy Newton had chosen the row behind, but he threw off his belt and moved to sit beside Caldwell.

The flight attendant was a dark woman with hair that had been buzzed short and dyed a very improbable blonde. She came to loom over the man beside Beverly; she bent over and tried to take the little box away from him. "I'll put this in the overhead compartment."

"No, ma'am, you won't."

"Perhaps you could put it under your seat. At least for takeoff."

"I'm going to hold on to it." He looked up at the flight attendant, and something in his eyes told her to drop it, to turn away.

Jimmy Newton asked, "So, Caldwell, what have you been up to? Where you been lately?"

Caldwell tried to think. Some images flew through his mind: there was a tropical island, maybe Fiji; New Zealand; some European city. He had no way of judging the newness of these memories. Then it occurred to him that he had some stale plane tickets in his pocket. He pulled them out and leafed through. "I was in Toronto," he said, which is where his financial advisers kept offices. "And Seattle. At least, Washington State. Went there for a little steelhead fishing."

"Bullfuck. Ingshit. You went there looking for lightning."

Caldwell nodded. "Maybe so. I like lightning."

"I don't," said Newton. "Lightning is like foreplay. I'm interested in getting fucked."

The engines howled, the little plane moved forward and, although it never seemed to achieve sufficient speed, somehow lifted into the air and ascended toward the sun.

Jimmy Newton droned on, the flat pitch of his voice sitting a quarter tone above the hum of the airplane's twin engines. It made Caldwell long to plug his ears. Newton was explaining something to do with the quantification of chaos, which, if successful, would enhance the dynamic modelling of weather systems a hundredfold. Caldwell disliked such talk, because it baffled him. True, he had once taught science, but only because budget cutbacks had forced everybody in the phys. ed. department to take on other duties. Caldwell had campaigned for geography; it seemed somehow *knowable,* since he could study atlases and learn how the world was stitched together. Instead he had been landed with grade nine science.

The curriculum for that level included work on weather. Caldwell had studied the teacher's guide and in the classroom bandied about words like "convection," "latent heat" and "potential energy." He explained, haltingly, how hurricanes were formed, how water in the ocean near Africa was heated by the sun and set into circular motion. When the students asked questions, he sought refuge in history. He would tell them what he remembered of Hazel, the storm that had killed thirty-five of his neighbours.

Jimmy Newton went on about this new prognostic technique, the quantification of chaos, but Caldwell didn't listen, he knew the science was far beyond him. The science was a little beyond Jimmy Newton, for that matter; he would often use technical terms and then add, "Or some such shit." But Newton didn't really need science in order to understand storms.

They called him Mr. Weather. Jimmy Newton was in the *Guinness Book of World Records*; he'd seen the most tornadoes, had the most personal experiences with cyclones—the umbrella term for both the western hemisphere's *hurricanes* and the eastern's *typhoons*. Newton was on television quite a bit, particularly a show called *Miami AM*. When a storm was headed toward Florida, Newton would tell the viewers what to expect. "This is only a one, it's barely maintaining status. You all can sleep through this one." Or he might say: "Okay, batten down the hatches. She's a three." When there was a storm somewhere other than Florida, Jimmy Newton would be unavailable (he'd be wherever the storm was), but he would appear on television afterwards, relating his experiences, showing his videos and photographs.

He enjoyed being recognized on the street. He liked it when children pointed at him and shouted, "It's Mr. Weather!" Newton had a low-grade ambition to be on that Oprah show, not so much because he liked it (or even had much familiarity with it), but more that he hated small potatoes. *Miami AM* was small potatoes, hosted by some juiced-up pretty boy and a woman with big boobs and hair.

Newton also had a website, hugely popular with weather weenies. He got thousands of hits a day, mostly from people interested in particular systems. He tried to monitor all of the active weather around the globe, and his projections and predictions were uncommonly accurate. The National Oceanic and Atmospheric Administration made no secret of the fact that they checked Jimmy Newton's website daily, that they at least factored his thinking into their data. Some of the hits Jimmy got were from people who had heard about his photographs and bits of video. He had a reputation for bravery, although it was more truly an utter recklessness. He would take his cameras into the storm, and record images of power and destruction unlike anything people had ever seen.

Newton abandoned the subject of chaos abruptly and pointed out the window. "You ever do this, Caldwell?"

"Do what?"

"We're in a cloud now, right?"

Caldwell turned and saw whiteness swimming by outside the airplane. "Right."

"Okay, so we wait, and . . . look, we're not in the cloud any more."

"Uh-huh?"

"But when did we leave? You know? You can never tell when you leave a cloud, you just know when you're out of it. Same the other way: you can never tell when you're going *into* a cloud, but then—"

"You know what, Jimmy? I'm a little tired. I think I'll try to get a little sleep."

Newton nodded. "Sure thing."

Caldwell turned away, pressing his forehead against the thick oval of plastic. The plane went inside a cloud.

One Saturday morning (back when Caldwell was a phys. ed. teacher forced to grapple with science) he had spread the paper out before him on the kitchen table. He read the sports section first, out of habit, registering scores from hockey and American college basketball. He then turned to the news proper, flipping the section over so that he could see the weather map. A front was advancing from the Prairies. The local forecast called for light snow. Caldwell jerked his head up, shot a glance through the kitchen window. *They blew it again,* he remarked to himself with some inner satisfaction. Already the snowfall was heavy enough to give the world outside a silvery glow.

He noticed the six numbers isolated in a tiny box in the top right-hand corner of the front page: 6 22 47 16 8 9. Oh, right, the lottery. He'd bought a ticket the day before, so he fished around in his pocket and drew it out. He had purchased it on little more than a whim; it would indeed have been precisely "on a whim" except that he did it quite often. Caldwell had no system or series of special numbers, he liked to leave chance where it belonged, in the hands of the gods. So he would ask for the store computer to decide for him, to spit out a coupon with six random numbers. He took out his ticket now and saw: 6 22 47 16 8 9.

Caldwell laid the ticket aside and drummed his fingers on the tabletop. The house was empty and for a moment he couldn't remember why. Then it came to him that Jaime had taken Andy to hockey practice, it was her turn, her week, and that was why he was allowed the luxury of having the Saturday paper spread out before him on the kitchen table.

He looked up at the clock. They would be heading back now, they would be halfway home. Caldwell picked up the telephone.

The first call he made—before he called his sister, before he called any of his close friends—was to Matty Benn. Jaime would have taken him to task on this. She would have demanded, "Why did you call that A-hole?"

Why, indeed? Caldwell had a number of reasons. For one thing, even if Matty Benn wasn't a close friend, he was a current friend. Caldwell now hung out more with Matty Benn than he did with his putative best friend, Denton MacAuley. He'd been with Benn the night before. They had met at Mystery's, something they did most Friday evenings. Caldwell and Matty Benn had consumed beer and shots of whisky and stared at the naked women.

And maybe Matty Benn was an A-hole—at Mystery's, for example, he hooted and spilled his drinks and yelled "Nice tatas!" every few seconds—but what Jaime didn't seem to realize was that Caldwell himself was an A-hole. He enjoyed the drinking too, and he could chime in with some very loud hoots.

Another reason was that Matty Benn was a reporter for the *Examiner,* he had the municipal beat. He reported on such things as had just happened to Caldwell, and as he picked out the numbers on the phone Caldwell could already imagine the headline: LOCAL MAN WINS MILLIONS. He could imagine the photograph: he would be holding an oversized cheque, and he would be smiling. Not grinning, not showing any of his slightly crooked teeth, only smiling slightly as if this were all a little prank pulled off by himself and the Big Man Upstairs. (The next day's front page would look nothing like this, of course. It would feature a small photograph of Caldwell climbing into a police car, his features obscured by falling snow.)

But the true reason Caldwell called Matty Benn is that Matty knew Darla Featherstone. Caldwell did not necessarily believe that Benn had slept with the Channel Four reporter, no matter how much detail Matty supplied whenever he told his stories. But Matty knew her, had access to her.

Caldwell did not want to sleep with Darla Featherstone— that was not the point. But when she'd first appeared on the Channel Four news a couple of years earlier, Caldwell thought she was an extraordinary-looking woman, perhaps the most attractive woman he'd ever seen. Darla Featherstone had a curious intermingling of bloodlines, something like Chinese, African and Swedish. Jaime, of course, did not. Jaime had generations of Canadian blood coursing through her body, her distant ancestors dour Scots who'd come over looking for severe conditions, something to truly test their mettle. Jaime was brawny—she'd been a champion swimmer—and Darla Featherstone was slight. If Caldwell had wanted to, he could list many points on which his wife and this woman, this image on the television screen, were opposites. Remarking on these differences was not wrong, was it?

Caldwell remembered sitting in the family room one night, reading yet another science textbook, trying to understand these riddles so that he might explain them to the hopeful children in his classroom. A voice on the television said something like, "And here with that story is Channel Four's Darla Featherstone."

Caldwell's head jerked up, and Jaime laughed from the sofa. "You like her," his wife chided gently.

"No, I don't," said Caldwell.

"Go on, admit it. You like her."

"No, I don't," lied Caldwell.

When Matty Benn answered the phone, Caldwell said, "I just won the lottery."

"Holy shitballs," said Matty. He asked a few questions and then said, "You know what? I'll call Darla."

"Good idea," said Caldwell. Caldwell the A-hole.

BEVERLY STARED THROUGH THE PLASTIC WINDOW at Dampier Cay, which seemed very small indeed. The island was shaped like a piece of macaroni, an idle reflection that made Beverly bury her face in her hands.

In the seat beside her, the immaculate man in the pure white shirt and crisp blue trousers shook his head in commiseration. "Yes," he declared. "What will be, will be."

Beverly had no response; she was paralyzed by so silly a thing as the thought of macaroni.

"And He alone knows what will be," said the man. He tightened his grip on the small cardboard box, his fingers strong and gleaming, as though they were made of bronze. "You know, I wrote the hundred-and-fifty-second sam."

Macaroni, remembered Beverly, *and not even real macaroni, rather something made from a packet of noodles and cheesy powder.*

"I used to say," continued the immaculate man, "that I had written the one-hundred-and-fifty-*first* sam, but then I heard that they found one in the desert. And it was written before mine, so mine is the hundred-and-fifty-*second* sam."

Margaret loved the stuff, which broke Beverly's heart. It broke Beverly's heart that Margaret could love so wholeheartedly the junk the world handed out; Margaret with her yellow plastic bowl, the design of fairies so worn by time that it was all but invisible, spooning macaroni into her mouth at a dizzying clip, pausing only to shout, "Yum yum, piggy's bum!"

"David wrote the first one hundred and fifty," continued the coffee-coloured man, and now Beverly turned toward him, not to listen, but to try to quiet him. His eyes were soft; very dark but soft nonetheless. "Then there was the one in the desert, and now there's mine. One hundred and fifty-*two*."

In those days, the macaroni days, Beverly was always dating. While Margaret ate mac and cheese in the kitchenette, Beverly would be dressing in the bedroom, deciding which outfit to wear. It is not that she was desperate for a lover, but she was desperate to find a father for Margaret. Margaret seemed to have been born with a drive toward normalcy, a longing for the quotidian and democratic, and had a hard time living with fatherlessness.

There were two types of men available for dates. One was born in Orillia, or a long-time resident, and knew something of Beverly's family history. This type of man assumed a high degree of sluttishness on her part, and a typical date ended, not with a little kiss on the cheek, but with the man yanking down his zipper and trying to force Beverly's hand inside. The other type was new to the town, and the date usually went much better. This type would telephone the next day, ask to see Beverly again. On that second date, something inside Beverly, a perverse inclination toward fairness, would cause her to relate the story of her early childhood. There were never any third dates.

"Oh!" said Beverly, suddenly understanding. *"Psalm."*

"That's right," nodded the immaculate man. "Sam."

"Well," asked Beverly, "how does it go?"

"'Oh, Lord,'" began the man, needing no further encour-
agement, "'sometimes it seems as though You are very far away
from us.'" He closed his eyes, the better to speak from memory.
"'You withhold from us Your bitter bosom. You give us not the
holy teat.'"

The fact that the immaculate man was crazy gave Beverly
comfort. It didn't alarm her to encounter people who had been
driven out into the wilderness. She mistrusted more the people
who clung to the pillars of civilization.

"Caldwell?"

Caldwell lifted his forehead from the plastic window and
swung around to look at Jimmy Newton.

"I didn't post the name of this island," said Newton.

"What?"

"On my website. I didn't tell anyone I was going to
Dampier Cay."

Caldwell nodded slightly, uncertain as to what Newton
was telling him. "Okay."

"That's why it's just us. Me and you. Although *she's* here.
That slut."

"Who?"

"That blonde bimbo," said Newton. "Back there."

Caldwell glanced over his shoulder, even though he knew
whom Jimmy was referring to. The woman sat with her head
bent slightly, her eyes closed. In the seat beside her, the man
had lifted one hand from the little cardboard box in order to
raise a finger into the air, a finger that pointed toward heaven

and trembled with either fury or fear. The man was speaking, but his words were lost in the roar of the engines.

"Is she a chaser?" asked Caldwell. "I've never seen her before."

"She came looking for 'nados one time."

"And why," wondered Caldwell, "are you calling her names?"

"You know what that chick did?" asked Jimmy Newton. "She balled Larry DeWitt."

"*Balled?* What are you, twelve years old?"

"Larry told me all about it. It was one of those tornado tours, you know, and I drove one van and Larry drove the other. And for six days there's *nothing,* I couldn't find a lick of wind stronger than a fart. Then on the last day, supercell. *Super*-supercell. Even I'm impressed, this thing is popping tornadoes like a bitch pops puppies. Okay, so this chick, for one thing, she has some kind of, I don't know, *episode.*"

"Episode?"

"I didn't really see it, I don't know, DeWitt just told me she went a little freaky. Anyway. Everyone goes back to the motel. Okay. So Larry's in the shower, you know, and that chick comes into his room. Right? Wearing a bathrobe that isn't even done up, everything's hanging out, and she tears the towel off Larry and grabs hold of his dick and they have this hot, steamy sex. And it's not like DeWitt was looking for it. She just came to him."

"Was the storm still going on?"

"What?"

"This all happened while the storm was going on?"

"Yeah. Sick or what?"

Caldwell shook his head, as though hoping that pieces might fall into place. "Didn't you ever want to do anything like that? You know? Something. With somebody. While the rest of the world was falling apart?"

"Umm . . . we got a negative on that, Houston."

"I thought you said you like to get fucked."

"Sure. But not by, you know, a human being."

"Oh."

"That was kind of a joke, Caldwell."

"Oh."

"Besides," said Jimmy Newton, "I know what you like to do. During storms. I've seen you."

"You've seen me?"

"Damn betchas. Now *that* is sick."

"Harmless."

"Dangerous."

"Not," said Caldwell, taking another look at the woman, "dangerous enough." She had covered her face with her hands, and her shoulders were shaking. The man beside her continued to speak, his finger raised even higher now, almost poking the overhead luggage racks.

Jimmy Newton said, "Anyway, I tried this thing I was telling you about, this quantification of chaos. What you do is, you take all the factors you know, right, the heat waves and the pressure and the relative effect of the Coriolis given the distance from the equator—you know, all the usual shit—and then you plug in these numbers, this formula, which is *chaos*. I thought it was going to blow the pooter, man, but after about seven hours the thing spits out a trajectory. I check maps, I come up with *Dampier Cay*. So I book a ticket, but I didn't post the name."

"Why not?"

Jimmy Newton shrugged. "I'm not sure. Maybe because it's a long shot."

"Uh-huh."

"Maybe because it's not."

"What does that mean?"

"When I'm in there, you know, right inside, it's like . . ." Newton held his hand up in front of his own face, his fingers spread and waggling. "It's like my guts go like this." Newton made a fist, so tightly that his knuckles turned white. "Okay? When I'm inside. But this time, as soon as I heard the name Dampier Cay . . ." Jimmy made the fist again. "This is gonna be something, Caldwell."

"So, what, you were worried about the others?"

"A little bit maybe. Mostly I wanted to keep it all to myself. Get in there with the camera, you know. Hey, I'll probably get on that Oprah show."

"Sure."

"Maybe get a profile on *60 Minutes*."

"Maybe."

"Maybe get my ass kicked through the Pearly Gates."

"What?"

"So you never explained, how did you get here?"

"Well . . ." Jimmy Newton didn't know about the problems Caldwell had with his memory. It's not so much that Caldwell was good at covering them up, more that Newton wasn't really interested in other people. Caldwell changed the subject, which is something he did quite a bit without even realizing he was doing it. "He was a pirate, you know."

"Who?"

"Dampier. William Dampier. The man the island is named for."

"Hmm. Isn't that fascinating? Hmm. No."

Caldwell thought about pirates a lot. Some of the trips he made were inspired only by the notion that such-and-such a place was once the haunt of cutthroats. Caldwell had cruised the Galapagos Islands, for example, and while everyone else on the yacht was fascinated by the wildlife (the marine iguanas, the prehistoric frigate birds, the pitiful flightless cormorants), Caldwell thought only about the Merry Boys. He imagined their ship, the *Batchelor's Delight,* moored in the shelter of a quiet bay. He pictured the buccaneers lying drunkenly ashore, beside the sea lions and lizards, their bodies naked, blistered and barnacled. What Caldwell loved about pirates was their relationship to their families, far away in Jolly Old. Because pirates did such horrible things, had such scabrous souls, they could afford to love deeply and it would not destroy them. And because their dear ones were so distant, this love could not hurt *them*.

THE PLANE LANDED on a strip that had been torn out of the coconut trees, and taxied toward a small wooden building. The flight attendant pressed the microphone to her lips. "Please remain seated," she chanted, "until the airplane comes to a complete stop."

No one listened. The immaculate man leapt to his feet and raced toward the exit. The two young women stood up and tore off their shirts; one wore a floral bikini top, the other a halter. They were grim-faced, but determined to have fun. Jimmy Newton fished his cameras and computer gear out of the luggage racks, the elderly couple rose—still holding hands—and moved into the aisle. Beverly stood up because everyone else did: do what other people are doing, so as not to attract attention.

Only Caldwell remained seated, staring through the little plastic window at the island. Then he shook his head, as though startled, and rose.

The stewardess popped open the door and people began to duck through. Beverly waited in the aisle for Caldwell to precede her, making a small gesture at him, at the exit. This seemed to baffle him. He stared at Beverly as though she were a foreigner, an alien. After a moment Beverly said, "Please," and Caldwell started into motion, grabbing the back of the chair in front of him and throwing his hips into the aisle.

At customs and immigration, a young fellow, no more than seventeen years of age, sat behind a crooked wooden desk. He accepted passports and declaration cards and asked what business people had on the island. The elderly couple said that they owned a vacation property and were coming to superintend should the storm hit.

The immigration lad nodded but seemed dissatisfied. He examined the passports of the elderly couple with interest. "You *own* this property?"

They both nodded, so slightly that, if need be, they could deny ever having done it.

"But where," persisted the boy in an officious manner, "is your primary residence?"

"For Christ's sake, Lancer," came a voice. "It's Mister and Missus Gilchrist. Now let everyone through so I can get my lot to the Edge."

The immigration boy began stamping passports.

The man who had spoken stood in the doorway, silhouetted by sunlight. Seeing that progress was being made, he turned, spat out a cigarette butt and disappeared.

They found him outside, standing beside a rusted minivan with the words *Water's Edge* stencilled onto its side. The man, tall and lean, wore white shorts and a T-shirt that bore his own likeness. A photograph had been transferred onto the material, and lettering underneath it announced, *Bonefish Maywell*. His skin was red from the sun, speckled and loose around the kneecaps and elbows. He wore a baseball cap, tugged down over his forehead, and sunglasses, so all that remained of his face was a burnished nose and a tiny mouth wrapped around a fresh cigarette. "Water's Edge, please," he intoned, motioning toward the minivan.

The immaculate man rushed forward, the cardboard box held out as an offering. Bonefish Maywell accepted it, and the other threw himself through the van's side door, scurrying toward the seats in the very rear. Maywell tossed the cardboard box through an opened side window, landing it neatly between the front captain's chairs.

The elderly couple wandered away, dragging their suitcases behind them, the little wheels sending up dust. Everyone remaining was destined for the Water's Edge. The overfed girls peeled off their jeans and stuffed them into travelling bags, which they then added to the top of their mountain of luggage. They wore thongs, and from behind they appeared to be wearing nothing at all. "How ya doin'?" one of them demanded of Maywell. The one who had worn glasses had removed them, so it was impossible to tell them apart. Both squinted in the harsh light.

"I'll deal with your luggage," said Maywell. "Please get into the truck, ma'am."

"Ma'am," repeated one of the girls. The other one giggled. They climbed into the van.

Jimmy Newton pointed at his own bags. "You be careful with this stuff, buddy-boy. If anything's broken, I'll know who to talk to."

Maywell stiffened, drew on his cigarette, managed a small nod. "I—" he began, or so it seemed. Caldwell realized that the man had said, "Aye," with a pirate's surly insolence. Maywell took hold of one of Jimmy's bags and lifted it upwards. Around the top of the vehicle was a roof rack, made of rusted pipe and fraying bungee cord. Caldwell threw his own sailor's duffel into this container. The man from the Water's Edge spun around quickly. "Not necessary, sir," he said. "My job."

Beverly also raised her own suitcase over her head and advanced toward the minivan. Maywell tossed away his cigarette and raised his arms as though in self-defence. "No, ma'am!" he barked, attempting to take the suitcase away from Beverly. "Let me do that."

"I can manage," said Beverly.

"*My* job, ma'am."

Beverly tossed the case. It landed half in, half out of the poorly constructed rack, but it stayed on top of the vehicle.

Bonefish Maywell, displeased now, threw the remaining bags on top of the van with irritated energy. He lit a new cigarette and got into the driver's seat.

Beverly realized that she was sweating, and she paused to consider her wardrobe, especially in light of the little the girls were now wearing. Beverly was dressed as she had been when she'd left Canada—a blue skirt and matching jacket, a white blouse, a camisole. She pulled off the jacket and then, after a moment's hesitation, unbuttoned and removed her blouse. She rolled up the clothes, tucked them in the crook of her arm. Beverly figured she still outstripped the overfed girls on the modesty front.

But as she climbed into the minivan, claiming the front passenger seat, she could sense Maywell stiffening. Beverly understood suddenly that she was wearing *underwear,* and even if she was less exposed than the girls, she was more provocative. Beverly often forgot that her body was still well formed, that her skin remained perfect, no matter the life she led—and she had led some odd lives. For two years, for instance, she had inhabited the same seedy tavern as her grandfather, sitting with him and his ancient cronies. She had laughed too loudly, wept and consumed grain alcohol, and when she abandoned that, she had attended Alcoholics Anonymous meetings in a church basement no less gloomy than the shadowy Dominion Tap Room. And yet, when she finally emerged, her skin glowed like a child's.

Another reason for Maywell's bristling, Beverly realized, was her seat selection. Beverly had claimed the front passenger's, even though there was space on the benches behind. She'd seen that it was free and jumped in, forgetting her place as a guest, forgetting herself maybe, thinking this was a chase somewhere in Oklahoma, that they were off core punching and it was her turn in the shotgun.

The sunburnt man turned the key in the ignition and the van howled before grudgingly turning over.

"Any word on the hurricane?" asked Beverly.

Maywell shrugged. "Plenty of words, ma'am. Not much that means anything."

The two girls asked, "Do you think it will hit this island?"

Maywell jerked his head upwards so that he was gazing into the rear-view mirror. "No. We're just a little island. No big storm's got business with Dampier Cay."

The coffee-coloured man spoke up from the seat in the rear. "What will be, will be."

"No it won't, Lester," said Maywell.

"Are there a lot of people staying at the Water's Edge?" wondered one of the girls.

"Not too many," admitted the driver. "There were some cancellations."

"So," interpreted the other girl, "there's not like a lot of guys there?"

"No, ma'am."

"Like how many?"

"There would be none, ma'am."

"*Ma'am*," scowled the girl, turning to look out the window. They were driving through Williamsville now, which consisted of a long cobblestone road fronted by a general store, a post office, a bar and two nearly empty gift shops.

Maywell was looking into the rear-view mirror, not really paying attention to the road ahead. Mind you, the inhabitants of the island knew him well, and whenever they saw the Water's Edge van they sought shelter in doorways, between buildings. "We had some last-minute cancellations," repeated Maywell, studying Caldwell and Jimmy Newton. "Of course," he said, swinging his head to stare at Beverly, "there were some last-minute *registrations* too."

"My name's Beverly." She had meant to say it civilly, even sweetly, but for some reason it issued forth with volume and an edge.

"Yes, ma'am."

One of the girls introduced herself as Gail and the other had a very odd name, Sorvig or something that sounded like that. They directed questions toward Maywell's back. "So you're pretty sure the hurricane's going to miss, huh?"

"Yes, ma'am."

"Ha!" barked Jimmy Newton, but then he pretended he hadn't, looking at Caldwell as though they were friends. The girls likewise pretended they hadn't heard him, and Sorvig put another question to Maywell.

"So you're not worried?"

"No, ma'am."

"How come?"

"Hurricanes are always headed towards more important places—Florida, Carolina—so they can make the national news at seven," he said.

"What about Fred?" asked Beverly.

"Ma'am?"

"Fred. October eighty-six. Seventeen dead on this island."

"I don't think you want to be talking about Fred, ma'am."

"Fred took my son," said Lester, the immaculate man.

They drove the rest of the way to the Water's Edge in silence.

Caldwell paid attention to none of this, because a memory was happening to him. He gazed out the window as though sightseeing, but his eyes, behind dark glasses, were soft and a little watery. The memory, which happened to Caldwell often, was of a man flying and smiling.

The man was Bob Janes, and Caldwell could recall a lot about him. He was the father of Kenny, Caldwell's childhood playmate. They had lived at 32 Raymore, and Mr. Janes was not at home when Hurricane Hazel came. He worked nights at Dominion Packers, and management, choosing to endorse only the weather report for "rain," insisted that he come work his shift. So Bob Janes had been away when his house and family were taken by the storm. He wasn't the only one: Eddie Ducammen worked at Dominion Packers too, and he lost his wife, his child and his mother. Afterwards, Eddie Ducammen disappeared, which was somehow judged right and proper. But Bob Janes remained in the neighbourhood, mostly at the New Leaf Restaurant, where he eschewed everything from the menu except the draught beer and bar shots. He was indulged in this. The man had lost his family, after all, and besides, everyone would much rather have Mr. Janes inside the New Leaf than walking the streets. Bob Janes had become a very nasty piece of business, hollering at people for little, or no, reason. Caldwell was fascinated by him.

The memory, then: Caldwell steps out of the corner store, a new Superman comic book tucked under his arm so that he can unwrap a few pieces of Double Bubble. Bob Janes is in the middle of Bloor Street, dodging traffic like a matador dodges bulls, swivelling his hips just enough to avoid getting hit. Then he loses his balance and falls backwards. A car, a red Edsel, smacks him, sends him flying through the air. Mr. Janes lands at the young Caldwell's feet. A halo of red spreads out around his head. And, Caldwell sees, the man is smiling.

BEVERLY WOKE FROM HER NAP with a start. She almost always woke with a start, something the professionals—the counsellors and doctors—said was atypical and therefore worthy of attention. But it was not atypical in her experience. Her grandfather usually sputtered to life already kicked into a state of advanced alarm, his lips formed around obscenities. And Margaret, her Margaret, had been visited by nightmares. Several times a night the child would bolt upright in her bed, shrieking as though she could keep the demons away simply with ear-bleeding pitch. The only person in Beverly's intimate acquaintance who passed peacefully from slumber was her ex-husband, Don Peabody.

Beverly took a look around and remembered where she was: Dampier Cay, the Water's Edge, cottage "K." The woman behind the check-in counter, Polly her name was, had assigned everybody quarters arbitrarily and rather imperiously. Gail and Sorvig were sharing a cabin halfway up the rise to the main building. When they asked if they could be closer to the beach, Polly shook her head, glancing at a clipboard as if to confirm the rightness of the declaration. Jimmy Newton was in A2, one of four apartments joined together in a squat row. "Just as long as it's got a lot of electrical outlets," he said. Polly didn't respond to this, she was busy giving the phys. ed. teacher the key to cottage "J."

"J" and "K" were actually the same cottage, with a wall running down the middle. Beverly suspected that the phys. ed. teacher's quarters were a mirror image of her own. She could hear him over there: he was sleeping, or at least trying to, and his bed groaned and squealed as he tossed.

Beverly supposed that he, like her, had poor sleep habits. That was about the only thing the professionals were agreed upon, that she had poor sleep habits. They worked hard on this, they prescribed pills and recommended regimens. Beverly threw away the pills and ignored the regimens. For example, what she had just done was verboten according to the pros. It was late afternoon, and instead of sleeping before dinner, she should have stuck it out until ten-thirty, which was the bedtime she was supposed to maintain. It saddened and angered Beverly that they denied her the wholesome pastime of napping, but such was her life. In the land of the damned, there is no nap time.

Beverly climbed out of bed and went to stare through the large window. Bushes and greenery pushed against the screen, as if the tendrils and leaves were seeking refuge. And perhaps they were, she thought; she vaguely believed in a spiritual confederation of life, with the most silent members—plants, animals, unborn children—in possession of the most profound knowledge. According to this theory—half baked, to be sure—the plants knew full well that the hurricane was coming, and pushed against the screen seeking communion.

Beverly went into the washroom and turned on the shower. The plastic stall stood in the middle of the tiny room, pushed into this odd position by a small tank and a complex arrangement of thick pipes.

One of the reasons Beverly had poor sleep habits was because Don Peabody had had proper ones. It was her own little act of resistance and rebellion. The professionals prided themselves on uncovering this ("You developed these odd sleeping patterns during your marriage? Interesting!"), but Beverly had never kept it a secret. During her marriage she purposefully stayed awake late, even if her eyelids were leaden. She arose early, even if every part of her, save a little pocket of perversity, wanted to stay in bed. It was a way of protesting Don's doglike attachment to the conventional.

Don Peabody embraced the ordinary, aspired to it as an ideal. When they were courting, for example, he had kissed her on the first date, felt her breast on the second, fingered her tentatively on the third and made love to her on the fourth. Then he proposed marriage. They honeymooned in Niagara Falls. Beverly went along with all this in a haze of incredulity that she was convinced was romantic love. She even enjoyed the conventionality, for a while.

But to Don Peabody the ordinary was a drug, and he was hopelessly addicted. Perhaps this explained a great deal about their daughter Margaret; perhaps there was a genetic component. Not that Beverly believed any such crock, but she was so soured by her trips to the professionals, constant and court-mandated, that she sometimes played their little games with caustic irony. So Beverly conjectured (in a manner only she found amusing, and even then not very) that she should never have wondered at her daughter's affinity for the conventional, seeing as the child was conceived during dutiful, straightforward intercourse on a heart-shaped mattress while Muzak poured down from tiny speakers in the ceiling.

What it all boiled down to (the professionals always wanted to boil things down, they were the witches of the new age) was this: Don Peabody lacked an imagination. He was incapable, therefore, of improvising his life. Don relied on cues and clues that he'd gather from various sources: television, magazines, perhaps the odd newspaper column. It was as though he were always taking straw votes and going along with the majority. When the honeymoon at Niagara Falls was over and they were living together in a two-bedroom rented condo, Don found himself somewhat at sea. He didn't seem to know how to proceed, how to conduct himself. He could only follow the charts. He went to work, he watched prime-time television, he went to bed at eleven. When Margaret was born, Don chucked her under the chin. That was the extent of his parental involvement, virtually all he could think of. He chucked the baby so much that Margaret began to scowl when he loomed near and turtle her shoulders into her ears. Still, everyone was reasonably happy—until Don recalled that there was one more thing he could do under the circumstances, something he'd seen on television, something he heard about a lot, something he'd seen his own father do. He left Beverly for another woman.

One of the pros, Dr. Herndorff, had asked, "Why do you think you married him in the first place?"

"Search me," Beverly replied, adding a large, melodramatic shrug for effect. She was opposed on general principles to the quest for truth and understanding. This was, however, an area in which she had a little insight. For one thing, Don was basically a nice man, because it takes imagination to be evil or perverse. More importantly, he was unable to extrapolate imaginatively from her origins, which meant that Don Peabody was basically the only eligible bachelor the town of Orillia had to offer.

The shower's controls were finicky. To avoid scalding herself, Beverly had to concentrate as though she were a pilot landing an airplane. She stood beneath the water with a hand on each knob, mixing hot and cold. A minute into the shower the hot water ran out. Beverly cranked the left-hand knob as far as it could go, but the spray turned first tepid and then cool. Beverly defiantly pulled the cake of soap from the dish, worked up a lather rubbing her goose-pimpled flesh. She threw the soap down between her feet and let the water strike her. It was now so cold that she was short of breath. How could the water be so cold? Surely on sun-baked Dampier Cay it would be easy to keep water hot. She thought about this to prevent herself from thinking about the icy ache that enveloped her body. She stood in the shower until all of the suds had gone down the drain, and then she stumbled out, laughing, a bright pink from the chill.

She glanced out the window then—which was not covered, the venetian blinds bundled together unevenly at the top of the frame—and saw Lester. He held gardening shears in his hands and was working on the council tree just outside the window, snipping away shoots from the gnarled branches. At least, Beverly gathered that's what he had been doing, but his labour was now arrested as he stared into her room.

Beverly turned away from the window. A hunger came upon her, a deep, general hunger, but as she stood there, letting the warm air steal away the numbness, trying to decide how to dress, the hunger crystallized. It was actually food she was hungry for. She hadn't eaten since . . . since when? Canada? Beverly started sorting through her suitcase and drew out a pair of shorts, hunter green and multi-pocketed, designed for an arduous trek through Ontario's hinterland. She put these on and then selected a plain white T-shirt, pulling it over her head, spinning as she did so, and when her head popped through she was staring out the window once more. Lester had disappeared.

She slid the big glass door to one side—a task that required considerable strength—and walked out into the world.

The twinned cottages "J" and "K" were near the water, closer than any other of the resort's buildings; she had only to walk across a gravel road and a patch of thistly growth to reach the beach. But they were the furthest from the rest of the complex. The resort ended just on the other side of "J" and "K." Beyond was a small church, made out of plywood and painted blue. Beside the church sat a tiny, crowded graveyard. There were many stones there, the names obscured by lichen. There were also simple crosses, two pieces of barnboard hammered together, a name neatly rendered with whitewash.

The Water's Edge was a collection of buildings clustered around a small cove. The office and restaurant occupied a long, low building atop a rise. Cabins and rows of maisonettes spread out from there. The rise led to a more substantial hill—Lester's Hump—but Beverly was not interested in high ground.

The water on the leeward side of the island was calm, shone the colour of emeralds and sparkled with the setting sun. As Beverly mounted the stone steps to the main building, she could hear the surf pounding on the windward. When she got to the top, she was drawn forward, past the main building and a patch of manicured lawn. She found herself standing on top of a cliff, twenty, maybe twenty-five feet high. Looking left and right, she saw a series of boulders, little caves, tiny lagoons. It would be easy enough to climb down the rock face, which, Beverly noticed, is what Gail and Sorvig had done.

The waves were large and loud, and the girls were romping about in the surf. They screamed and giggled as salt water licked their bodies. Thirty feet beyond them, Beverly saw, a dark shape moved through the surf, a shark, relentless and lonely.

Beverly waved at the girls in a friendly fashion and went in for dinner.

CALDWELL COULD NOT GET COMFORTABLE, not that he expected to, or even deserved to. He tried various positions: on his back with hands laced together behind his head, curled on his side with both arms driven between his legs. He even tried the other bed, for there were two singles in cottage "J," at right angles to each other. Caldwell wondered what situation might demand this alignment, what union or family would want to sleep like that, heads close together but bodies divided so they could never meet.

He could hear the woman in the room beside his. She was pounding about fairly heavily, and making little drumming noises, *Bum-bum-bum*. This was one thin wall; Caldwell suspected that a fart would rent it asunder. He heard a hissing sound then, water splashing. A series of images occurred to him, and he allowed them to pass without interference. He did not recognize all of the naked women in his mind's eye, but then came an image he knew well, a woman with oversized thighs and breasts made to look plastic by wet Lycra. Caldwell closed his eyes and listened to the pounding of the surf. It began gently enough, but soon the noise, the roaring and the thumping, became almost unbearable. It sounded, thought Caldwell, as though a streetcar trestle had been torn loose and was battering at the very foundations. And he fell into the hole once again, the hole in the middle of his life.

He had said, "Good idea," to Matty Benn's suggestion that he call Darla Featherstone. After he hung up, Caldwell cradled the telephone and didn't move from beside it. He sat with his hands on his knees, his fingers gripping so tightly that blood left them. He made no further phone calls, even though this was monumental news. Caldwell didn't earn much as a teacher, and he squandered what little he had. He didn't know exactly *how* he squandered it, because his hobbies and habits were not extravagant. He enjoyed fishing, owned a fourteen-foot boat with a twenty-five-horsepower motor, but this was nothing, he had seen teenage boys out on Lake Simcoe with huge glittering bass boats, four-stroke engines as large as pagan idols. He played poker every couple of weeks, but just dollar, two-dollar stakes. There were, of course, the Friday-night visits to Mystery's, where Caldwell would drink too many beers and purchase a table dance or two. Still, it was always only a dance or two. No, Caldwell did not know where his money went. It seemed to get picked up like leaves by the wind, blown out of his yard and into someone else's.

When the phone finally rang, Caldwell knew who it was. He lifted the receiver and said, "Hello," in what he hoped was an intelligent or mysterious way, almost making a melody of the two syllables.

"Is it true?"

"Yeah. I guess so. I've got the ticket with the numbers."

"You have to go down to the lottery office. No, no. Wait. This is better. We'll come to your house, we'll film you with the ticket, right, then we'll film you going down—are you sure the numbers are right?"

"Yes. Quite sure." Caldwell felt as though he were watching himself on television.

"Okay, okay, excellent. Look, I've got to round up a cameraman. It's Saturday. *Fuck.* Give me your address."

Caldwell did so, and even began giving instructions, but Darla Featherstone cut him off. "I know the street. How big a burg do you think this is?"

She was right. In his head Caldwell had been briefly inhabiting some other city, some cosmopolis full of purlieus and quarters, a place large enough to allow the *possibility* of an illicit love affair. But all it took was Darla Featherstone's saying, "I know the street," to drive that notion out of his mind. That was as close as he came to unfaithfulness. But the wheels were already in motion. Something like a hurricane. Caldwell had thought about this, many times. A hurricane begins with the sun resting on the water, the two meeting as sun and water should.

"Okay," said Darla Featherstone, "don't move a muscle. Sit tight. I'm going to round up a cameraman and—*fuck,* it's really coming down out there."

He glanced out his window, and saw nothing but whiteness.

Caldwell came back to himself with a start, alarmed by a sound from cottage "K," a pained grunt. He heard a glass door being slid back into place, and understood that the woman next door had left her room.

She was one of the women he had seen naked in his mind; oddly, the image seemed more an actual memory than many of the others did. *I've done what you just did,* this woman had said to him. Caldwell swung his legs off the thin mattress. "Like hell you have," he said aloud, and he decided that he needed to eat, that he was, in fact, ravenous. He pulled open his own sliding glass door—he too gave out a little grunt—and headed for the main building.

As he passed the small row of maisonettes, he heard his name called. Peering through a screened window, he saw Jimmy Newton sitting at a small table, in front of a small laptop, its screen providing the only light in a room that was unaccountably gloomy. The laptop was wired to paraphernalia, an odd little metal tower, a small sleek printer. There were pieces of paper everywhere, on the floor, the bed, even in the small sink in the corner. These were images of the storm as seen from heaven. Three were tacked to the wall.

Jimmy Newton had a cellphone pressed to his ear, and five more lay at his feet. Newton muttered, "Jesus H. Christ," and dropped this one down there too. "I pay for every damn system there is," he snarled. "You'd think one of the fuckers would work."

"Who are you trying to call?" Caldwell knew that Newton had no family, it was one of the things he appreciated most about him.

"I want to talk to someone at en-oh-double-eh. I need to know if they're thinking what I'm thinking." Newton had one more little phone to try. He flipped it open, put it to his ear. He didn't even bother pressing any of the buttons. He threw the thing away and muttered, "Talk about a dead zone."

"Can't get through to anybody?"

"I got the computer hooked up. Gee-ess-em. I'm bouncing off satellites, baby. But here on the third stone from the sun, you and I are sitting in a black hole. You know what? This is officially the armpit of the world."

"Huh. So he found it."

"You want to try making sense, Caldwell?"

"William Dampier. He and his Merry Boys sailed around the world, you know, looking for the ends of the earth. The end of the earth. So now you're telling me this is it. He found it."

"Christ," muttered Jimmy Newton, shaking his head. "I'm surrounded by lunatics here."

"You hungry? You want to get some dinner?" Caldwell could not have said why, exactly, but he craved company.

"Gimme a sec." Jimmy stabbed at the return button on his keyboard, leant back and watched as a new image appeared on the screen. Caldwell couldn't see it from where he stood, but the computer screen pulsated.

"Oh-oh," said Jimmy Newton.

"What?"

"I'm looking at the new NOGAPS. It looks a lot like the UKMET."

"I have no idea what you're talking about."

"You know. Global baroclinic readings." Newton rose from his seat, stretched, pulled material away from his crotch. "What the hell kind of chaser are you, anyway?"

"No kind," admitted Caldwell.

"That's right, isn't it?" Jimmy Newton pushed through the door of Unit A2, joined Caldwell outside. "Whereas I am some kind of chaser. What kind? Piss poor."

"What do you mean?"

"I mean, it looks like she's deflecting."

"Hmm?"

"The *storm,* numbnuts. Remember? The hurricane that we spent hundreds of dollars trying to get to? She's deflecting."

"Huh."

"Right now the best track puts her maybe four hundred miles north. *Koo-bah.* We should have gone to Cuba. Cuba is a lot more fun than this fucking place, anyway. It's got better booze and naked dancing girls. Fuck. We missed, Caldwell."

Caldwell had experienced misses before, plenty of them. He could simply have chosen to live on Guam, which is battered by more storms than anywhere else on the planet, but Caldwell liked to keep moving, like the sharks that shadowed the beach. "Oh, well," he said. "I don't really care. You know me. I just come for the fishing."

They entered the main building, went by the registration desk and into the dining room. Polly met them with a stern look on her face. "You're late," she said.

"Sorry," said Caldwell, but Jimmy Newton was less apologetic. He pretended to dig around in the pockets of his white shorts. "Hey, it's okay, lady, I got a note from my fricking *mommy.*"

"It's just that there's a schedule," Polly explained. She was in her mid-forties, pretty but almost trying not to be. Her hair, a light golden colour, was tied back so severely that it seemed to stretch the skin on her forehead. "The cook goes home at seven."

"Sorry," repeated Caldwell.

"Now listen," said Jimmy Newton, but then he fell silent. Maywell Hope was standing nearby, in a passageway that separated the restaurant from the resort's bar. He had a cigarette in the corner of his mouth, which made him squint, darkening his eyes. Newton looked back at Polly and nodded slightly. "Yeah, we're sorry."

Polly led them to a table and slipped menus onto the plastic placemats. The blonde woman sat nearby and was speaking to the two girls at a neighbouring table. The girls still wore their bathing suits and had soggy towels draped over their shoulders.

"You have to be careful of the undertow," she said. "Even strong swimmers are often powerless against it."

From his seat Caldwell could see the blonde woman in profile. Her nose was a little bit snubbed—a clinical observation, which is all Caldwell had been making for the past few years. She had shoved her plate of food away—the salad looked intact—and was drinking coffee.

"At Acapulco Bay in Mexico," she said, "twenty-four swimmers disappeared once, within a few seconds, all taken away by the undertow."

"Well," said Gail, "it's a good thing we're not in Acapulco."

The blonde woman nodded. "We're not in Acapulco."

Beverly had once planned to go to Mexico with Margaret. She had purchased an all-inclusive package, airfare and hotel, two meals a day, at a resort named Vista Playa de Oro in Manzanillo. The trip had, in a sense, been Margaret's idea. When the little girl started school, it hadn't taken her long to determine that the typical annual routine included a trip south during spring break. Margaret had no clear sense of what lay south; as far as she was concerned, there might be serpent-filled seas. All she knew was, most kids went away during the winter, and Margaret, fatherless and belonging to a mother branded with the mark of a particularly squalid devil, was determined to join those ranks.

Beverly hadn't managed to put anything together for that first year, when Margaret was in kindergarten, but the kid was so morose for the entire vacation that Beverly determined to do better. She took a second job, bagging groceries at Pilmer's Grocery on Tuesday and Thursday nights. She enjoyed that job, although she was not very good at it. Each conveyor belt of foodstuffs seemed a puzzle, a twisted mystery. Beverly would bite her tongue with concentration and try to visualize how to pack it most economically, but there was always a jar of instant coffee or something left lying in the catch-all. Beverly would take it and make vague feints at the stuffed plastic. Finally, she would shrug and hand the jar to the customer.

She lasted at the job because she was pleasant and, Beverly supposed, because Mr. Pilmer felt sorry for her. She saved up enough for the trip, did the research and located the least expensive resort. She had the whole thing arranged by early fall, and Margaret had weeks of feeling normal in at least this tiny regard. Beverly even found herself looking forward to the trip. She put the brochure about Vista Playa de Oro in the washroom with the old *House & Garden* magazines. Every so often she would open it and review the amenities and activities.

One night, she noticed an odd sentence sitting in the middle of a paragraph about water sports: *sometimes there is a strong undertow.* Of course, she'd seen that sentence before—she'd read the brochure countless times—but caught up perhaps in Margaret's childish enthusiasm, she'd been interpreting this as another selling point. *A strong undertow* was perhaps a condition favoured by surfers or fishermen. The truth made her skin go clammy. *A strong undertow* meant: *There is a monster in the water and it wants to steal your child.*

She went to the library the next afternoon, in order to research undertows. The public library was staffed by three elderly ladies, and as soon as Beverly mentioned the subject of *undertows,* they began a litany of horror stories, an eerie chant of warning. But the library's card catalogue didn't turn up any actual books on the subject.

Seeking credible information, Beverly made a phone call to her high school science teacher, Mr. Hardy. She used her married name when she said hello, so Mr. Hardy did not remember her at first. When she said her maiden name, Mr. Hardy went silent for a long moment. Then he said, "Yes, Beverly?" very pleasantly.

Beverly used to make Mr. Hardy uncomfortable, but she had hoped he'd got over it in ten-plus years. She made him uncomfortable on a lot of different accounts. For one thing, he'd been friends with her mother, had grown up on the same street, attended the same schools. So Mr. Hardy was not only aware of what had happened to Beverly's mother—everyone in town was *aware*—but he could count it as a personal loss. Mr. Hardy also felt uncomfortable because, in chemistry class, he would often come and stand over Beverly as she worked at the microscope. He would ask how she was coming along and spy down her shirt front. He gave Beverly very high marks, but it all made him very uncomfortable, and apparently still did, because he repeated:

"Yes, Beverly?"

"Do you know anything about undertows?"

"Excuse me?"

"Undertows." Beverly spoke with as much precision as she could muster.

"Beverly, I'm not really following you."

Beverly explained that she had arranged a holiday for her daughter but was now very frightened by the idea of undertows.

"Uh-huh. But what can I do for you?"

Beverly claimed she didn't know and rang off, but she was angry, because she *did* know. Mr. Hard-on was a science teacher, after all. He could tell her whether or not science could battle such things, whether or not knowledge could vanquish the undertow. She read his reaction as negative, so if knowledge was not the ticket, preparation was.

When they went to Coronation Park on a hot summer's day, Margaret would paddle about in the water like any small child. She could even swim, after a fashion, although it was very idiosyncratic; she would keep her arms at her side and propel herself forward by kicking. When she needed air, she would wave her hands briefly in front of her, making her head bob up. It was strangely graceful, Margaret's swimming, and reminded Beverly of some aquatic animal. An otter, perhaps, especially since Margaret wore a bathing cap to contain her long golden hair, and her head looked bald and sleek. But the undertow was waiting for little girls who'd learned to swim in tame Canadian bays and inlets. So Beverly got on the telephone and started inquiring about swimming lessons.

Beverly looked up. Everyone in the dining room was staring at her, and she wondered if she'd made a sound. Maybe she'd let down her guard and a moan had escaped her. Beverly suspected this was the case, because when she met their eyes, they looked away. Gail and Sorvig returned their attention to their desserts, Maywell Hope withdrew into the bar proper, Polly went over to a little table and dealt with a coffee urn, and Jimmy Newton concentrated on pouring the dregs of his Coke can into a glass.

The phys. ed. teacher, though, had finally removed his sunglasses and was staring at her. His eyes were blue, blue as a cloudless sky. The colour reminded Beverly of a scientific fact, one of a handful she'd managed to retain: even if the sky is empty, clear all the way to heaven, there is still potential rain there, enough for a deluge.

JAIME AND ANDY GOT HOME a few minutes after Caldwell had hung up. He hadn't moved off the white stool beside the wall phone, but sat there staring through the window at the falling snow. The flakes were becoming thuggish, pounding against the pane and making it rattle.

Jaime bounded up the half-stairs from the mud room with her coat still on—having kicked off her boots—and began to water the plants that were collected on the countertops. Snow was on her shoulders, in her hair, melting now and making her glisten. The flakes were huge and intricately fashioned, lake-effect snow blowing off the big bay. Caldwell's wife always got back from hockey practice full of industry and energy. The plant-watering was part rebuke, albeit a good-natured one. It was something both husband and wife did, coming back from hockey practice with ever more little chores to perform, making the other feel guilty. Which the other would, obligingly, not very convincingly.

Andy came to the kitchen table and flipped open the newspaper, finding the scores from last night's hockey games. He studied them intently. The kid could not retain multiplication tables, but name any player in the NHL and he could rattle off goals and assists; name one of his favourites and he could recite shot percentages and penalty minutes; name one of his heroes and Andy would go through the entire career, commencing with Junior B. Andy knelt on a chair, his hands banded across his forehead to keep his hair out of his blue eyes. For a long moment there was silence, and Caldwell didn't suspect it was the last moment of peace he would ever know.

The silence registered on Jaime, who straightened up from her watering, a look of concern on her face. "What's up?" she demanded. She shook her arms and shrugged her shoulders, dropping her coat onto the kitchen floor. As clothes became useless for any reason—if she no longer needed their warmth, if she wanted to be naked—she would throw them off wherever she stood.

"Lemieux got a hat trick," said Andy.

"What's up is," said Caldwell carefully, "we're rich."

When Jaime encountered a sentence she didn't understand, her reaction was to bristle, to furrow her brow. She would search the deliverer's eyes for enlightenment. This is what she did now, looking deeply into Caldwell, trying to see what lay in there. "Okay," she said finally, relaxing, "what the heck are you talking about?"

She began to remove her sweatshirt—it announced the existence of the Barrie Berries, a women's hockey team that Jaime played goal for—yanking up her undershirt in the process, so that for an instant Caldwell saw his wife's breasts.

"What I'm talking about is . . ." Caldwell snapped his fingers, making the thick paper pop. He didn't know how long he'd been holding the ticket. "We won the lottery."

"Bullwhip." Jaime didn't swear, wouldn't say "shit" if she stepped in it. She had a repertoire of tamer stuff: "bullwhip," "fudge," "cheesy cripes" and, of course, "A-hole."

Caldwell held out the ticket with a hand that shook slightly. "Son," he said—Andy jerked his head up from the statistics only then, apparently the statement "we're rich" had made little impact on him—"son, do you see those numbers at the top of the front page?"

Andy found the right page, dragged it across the table. He spotted the numbers and, collapsed over his folded arms, read them aloud. Jaime took a few steps forward so that the ticket pulled into focus, and when the last of the six numbers was read aloud, she shrieked. "What do we have to do, what do we have to do, we have to—" Jaime stopped suddenly. "Did you call your mother?"

Caldwell's shoulders sank suddenly. "No."

"Why not?"

Not because his first thoughts were of Darla Featherstone. No, Caldwell hadn't called his mother because, well, he could legitimately claim some concern for her fragile health, her brittle mental faculties. Caldwell's mother wandered through the hallways of a private nursing home, all leathery wrinkles in a fuzzy housecoat. Her nervous system was faulty, the wiring frayed, allowing her no moments of respite. News of this magnitude might well cause an overload, make her fizzle, spark, rattle, and come to a dead stop. Plus, Caldwell just plain didn't get along with her. He tried to avoid the subject, addressing the first of Jaime's questions, even though it had not been completed. "I have to go down to the lottery office."

"Check."

"Oh, but . . ." Caldwell laughed lightly. "There's a news

crew coming over here. They want to film me, you know, leaving to go down to the place."

"Why?"

"Well, you know . . ."

Jaime thought about it briefly, decided she didn't care, shrugged her shoulders and advanced on Caldwell. Caldwell braced, unsure of his wife's intentions. Jaime reached out and took the telephone receiver from its cradle beside his head, started poking out numbers on the touchpad. "I'm calling your mother," she said.

Jaime got along well with Caldwell's mother. She'd got along well with Caldwell's father too, had been able to converse with him when he was dying of lung cancer and all Caldwell saw was a shrivelled, nicotine-stained creature with no interest in anything.

"Mrs. Caldwell, please," Jaime said into the phone. As they went to seek the ancient woman, she turned and asked, "Where's the lottery office?"

"Right down on Simcoe. In the bank building." Caldwell was surprised at his sure knowledge. He supposed he'd noticed the logo on one of the dark windows of the town's one true skyscraper. Or he might more properly have *noted* it, in some clairvoyant expectation of this day.

"Hi, Mom," said Jaime. "Here's your bouncing baby boy." Jaime held out the receiver toward Caldwell, who accepted it, but only after a long moment. "Mom?"

"Has there been an accident?" Mrs. Caldwell demanded. That had been her reaction to the unusual all her life. If a relative should appear unexpectedly at the doorstep, even during a festive season, even bearing gifts and bottles of liquor, Mrs. Caldwell would demand, "Has there been an accident?" The irony being, of course, that there never had been an accident, a calamitous event, not in all her many years, just a slow, steady decline.

Caldwell said, "I won the lottery!"

"My husband Fred won the lottery once," she replied. "He won ten thousand dollars. He took me on my dream vacation." None of this had happened. Caldwell's father had once won a *thousand* dollars, had been so excited that he'd called his son and indeed announced plans for a dream vacation, but in the end, Caldwell suspected, the money just went into the cigarette fund.

Caldwell pretended he could have a normal conversation with his mother. "Yeah, well, hey, I won just a *little* bit more than that." His mother fell silent, and he rushed to fill the quiet. "I won about sixteen million dollars."

Jaime began to cough like Lou Costello, pounding on her chest with a fist, trying to force out the first syllable in the phrase "sixteen million dollars."

"Oh," said Mrs. Caldwell. "Yes, that is more than ten thousand. Are you taking me on a dream vacation?"

"I sure as hell am," Caldwell said enthusiastically. He wondered where his mother might want to go, but was afraid to ask.

Jaime grabbed the receiver away and started making plans. "Okay. I'm coming to pick you up. Caldwell's got to wait here for a cameraman or something. So me and Andy will come get you, and we'll meet him downtown at the lottery office and then we'll have the biggest breakfast in the history of breakfast. Are you in?"

Jaime nodded at some reply Caldwell's mother made, although Caldwell couldn't imagine it being more elaborate than a grunt. She replaced the receiver, gave her husband a kiss and started regathering her things. "Come, young Andrew," she said grandly, "we must go claim the *monah*."

"Can I get a new Game Boy?" asked Andy shyly.

"Son," said Caldwell, "you can have a *hundred* Game Boys. Not to mention a Game Girl. We is rich folk."

"I," said Jaime, "think I must be dreaming. Except that Antonio Banderas isn't hanging around naked, so maybe this is happening after all. Is it, Caldwell? Is it really happening?"

"Yeah," he nodded, "it's really happening."

Beverly drove to the YMCA, which stood upon a hill on the outskirts of town. It was late afternoon and the sun was dropping behind the building, turning it into a hard, hulking shadow. Margaret sat in the seat beside her, twisting the knob on the radio, searching for news, weather and traffic reports from Toronto, a hundred kilometres to the south. Margaret resented the fact that they lived in Orillia, a town of only a few thousand citizens. Millions lived in the megacity, Margaret had found out, so she wanted to live there too. But she couldn't, because her mother was bound to the little town in some way that Margaret couldn't begin to fathom.

They entered the building and Beverly's first thought was that it looked like a hospital. The walls were clean, there was a long reception desk and behind it several young people wearing white shirts. It looked more like a hospital than the local hospital did. Beverly knew the hospital very well from driving her grandfather there in the middle of many nights. He woke up dying at least twice a month; he would call Beverly and demand he be taken to Emerge. He always wore his housecoat, never belted tightly enough, and wandered into the registration area with the robe gaping open. They would wait much of the night—Beverly leafing through ancient news magazines—and then a doctor would once again tell the old man that he was just an alcoholic, that he wasn't dying yet.

He was still alive, in fact. He lived in a gloomy apartment and was cared for by an immense woman named Nancy, who believed, thanks to a diet of booze and prescription drugs, that Beverly's grandfather had money and that she would be rewarded handsomely at the time of his death. Beverly went over for dinner sometimes, and she and her grandfather fought bitterly. That was about the only fun the old man ever had these days.

The young people in white shirts wanted quite a bit of money for a family membership at the Y, but Beverly didn't blink an eye, she ponied up, writing cheques that emptied both her accounts, making up the shortfall from money she'd collected in the Dream Jar. As soon as they received their picture IDs, Beverly asked about swimming lessons. *Oh,* they said, *you want to talk to Steve.*

Steve appeared, a tall, tanned young man. He had a swimmer's body and a nice smile. Arrangements were made to give Margaret swimming lessons on Thursday evenings and Sunday afternoons. Beverly thought that was inadequate, but there were no more openings. Steve told her not to worry, Margaret could always come to free swims and practice.

After the third lesson, Steve delivered Margaret into Beverly's hands and asked her if she wanted to go out on a date. Beverly was flattered, if for no other reason than Steve was a lot younger than she was (by almost nine years, as things turned out).

Steve was a nice guy. He was a good listener, nodding with sympathy, never interrupting, twisting his head so that he might hear better. At first Beverly thought there was something wrong with one ear, but she noticed over time that Steve was as likely to twist his head one way as the other. *Water,* she realized. His ears were always plugged with pool water.

Here's how nice a guy he was: On their third date, she began to speak of her early childhood, of Gerald and Brenda. It was the only time Steve ever cut her off. "Oh yeah, right," he said. "Some guys told me about that. Weird, huh?" Then he resumed carving up his steak. *You, young man,* thought Beverly, *are having big sex tonight.*

Margaret started campaigning for marriage very early in the courtship. And Beverly didn't quash the girl's dreams. She only said, "We'll see what happens," or, "Give it time, give it time."

There were a few weeks that were as good as mother and daughter ever knew. Except for the actual swimming lessons part. Steve told Margaret to forget all about her idiosyncratic swimming style. She did so immediately. The first thing she seemed to learn was how to sink to the bottom of the pool in a very alarming fashion. Beverly mentioned this to Steve, before any of the dating, and he only said, "Don't worry."

Steve always said *Don't worry.* He didn't worry about anything himself, and he didn't truly comprehend that other people might. So, for example, when he and Beverly first had sex, Steve pushed her back onto the mattress and whispered, "Don't worry." He offered no explanation as to why she shouldn't worry, if he was sterile or prescient or if he intended that they should wed or what.

But Beverly did worry, about a lot of things, especially the damned undertow. Week after week, Beverly watched the pool through a huge window in the YMCA's lobby. Margaret's crawl was a childish dog-paddle, her limbs crooked, her head bobbing above the surface. Steve attempted to teach her the breaststroke, but Margaret's arms, twig-thin and rubbery, could not lift her upper body, and her kick propelled her toward the bottom like a tiny pink submarine.

As time passed, the world outside turned naked and cold. Inside the YMCA it was perpetually subtropical, but Beverly drove through all sorts of hellish weather so that Margaret would not be taken by the undertow. Once, Beverly drove her daughter through an early season storm that was actually responsible for three deaths. She didn't even think about it, just drove through the wind and ice toward the YMCA.

THE PIRATE'S LAIR was a long room adjacent to the dining area, with large windows that looked out on the leeward side of Dampier Cay, the little cove where three small craft were moored. After dinner, people drifted into it, Maywell Hope first, because he did duty as bartender. He was surprised to find Lester at the bar, his golden hands folded together as though he were trying to hide the bottle of beer there. Maywell stopped and stared at Lester for a long moment. Then he threw open the hinged leaf, stepped behind and began to rinse out glasses. Finally he asked, "Did you mark that one down, Lester?"

"Yes, sir, I marked it down. I'm not a thief."

Gail and Sorvig came in next, heralded by laughter. They were animated and loud, never abandoning their hope that someplace on the damned island there was something going on. Their faces fell as they entered the lounge. They sat down at a little table and asked Maywell, a bit petulantly, if he knew how to mix a Boston Cooler.

"No, ma'am."

"*Ma'am*," Gail repeated, half amused, half pissed off. "How's about a Cocomacoque?"

Maywell shook his head.

Gail looked at the liquor bottles arrayed behind Maywell Hope. "Tell you what," she said. "Why don't you just pour that top shelf into a pail?"

"I'll make you the house specialty," said Maywell.

"What's it called?"

"It's called the House Specialty, ma'am."

"Ma'am," chorused both girls as Maywell began to mix their drinks.

Jimmy Newton and Caldwell arrived, climbing aboard stools at the long bar. Newton pointed toward a corner of the room. "Hey. A television."

Maywell glanced up from his drink preparations. "True," he said. "That's what it is."

"You know what's amazing?" said Jimmy Newton. "You hit the little button that says *power* there, the screen fills up with all these dots of light, and they actually form *images.*"

"Here at the Water's Edge, sir, we encourage conversation."

"You encourage conversation?"

"Uh-yuh," Maywell grunted. "That I do."

Polly appeared, reached behind the bar to retrieve a rag and immediately began wiping the table where the girls sat. Sorvig told her, "He won't let us watch television."

Polly looked at the man behind the bar. "May?"

"It's the first night," said Maywell, slapping two house specialties on the bar before him. "Everyone's supposed to get to know each other. What can I get you to drink?" he demanded of Newton and Caldwell.

"Beer," answered Jimmy.

"What kind?"

"I don't care. I'll try the local donkey piss."

"If the guests want to watch television . . ." began Polly.

"There's never anything on the television but foolishness," argued Maywell. "It'd be best if they talked, you know. Got to know each other."

"Where are you from?" Gail demanded of Maywell Hope.

Maywell shrugged, tugged the brim of his baseball cap lower. "Around."

"I'm from Orillia, Ontario," said a voice. Beverly stepped carefully over the threshold into the Pirate's Lair.

"There you go," said Maywell. "And what can I get you to drink?"

"I don't drink," said Beverly. "I'm an alcoholic."

Lester said, "I'll have a beer and a glass of rum."

"You'll have another *beer,* Lester, and you'll be happy to get it."

"What school of bartending did *you* go to?" wondered Sorvig.

Maywell ignored her, addressed Beverly. "Perhaps you'd like a glass of pineapple juice."

"Yes," she agreed.

"And sir?"

Caldwell looked at the liquor bottles. "I'd take some of that single malt. With a bit of ice. Please."

"I'm from Orillia, Ontario," repeated Beverly, getting on the stool beside Caldwell. "Which makes me Canadian. I noticed that you have a Canadian passport."

"Right," said Caldwell. There was a silent moment then; everyone expected the man to say more.

"This 'getting to know each other' is really not working out," commented Gail.

"Let's turn on the TV," said Sorvig.

"I don't see why I can't have a rum," argued Lester. "Miss Polly? May I please have a small glass of rum?"

"Lester, think about all the times you've specifically told me *not* to give you any rum."

"But I didn't mean *now*, Miss Polly."

Maywell presented Beverly with a glass of pineapple juice. She had a sip, licked her lips with appreciation and then said, "Mr. Hope, why don't you tell us some of the fascinating history of Dampier Cay?"

Caldwell couldn't tell if the woman was for real or not. Neither could Maywell, who spent a long moment staring into her eyes, searching for mockery or condescension. Apparently he couldn't find any, because he shrugged and stated, "Well, it's called Dampier Cay after William Dampier, who was sent out to sea as the Queen's official cartographer but took up pirating as a sideline. I expect because it was fun. William Dampier and his crew, the Merry Boys."

"Any of those pirates still around?" asked Sorvig.

Maywell nodded. "There's some." There was nothing in his voice to suggest that the answer was flip or ironic.

"'Cause really," said Gail, "we'd like to meet one."

"All the guys where we work are tweezoks," said Sorvig. "A pirate sounds just about right."

"A pirate," said Gail, "wouldn't freak and fuck off just 'cause of a storm on the way."

"Amen to that," intoned Sorvig. They raised their glasses and clinked them together.

"Let me guess," said Beverly, aiming a finger at Maywell

Hope. "You're a Merry Boy. Your, what, great-great-great-great-great-grandfather . . . ?"

Maywell shrugged. "Something like that."

". . . sailed with this William Dampier. That *is* fascinating."

"Perhaps." Maywell was noncommittal. "The Merry Boys took wives from the islands, you know, which is why there are so many coffee-with-cream-coloured, like Lester. What's interesting is that I have no black blood in me. My great-great-whatever-grandmother must have come on the ship with Dampier."

"Sailing around on a ship full of pirates," said Gail. "That sounds just about right."

Beverly spun around on her stool. "What do you two do?" she asked.

"What we do is—" began Gail.

"—work for a cable network," finished Sorvig.

"Planet Man, it's called."

"Yeah, only we call it Planet Dickhead."

No one understood what the girls were talking about, so no one said anything for a few moments.

"It's a television network," Sorvig said, "for guys."

Gail continued, "It's got sports and shows where dickheads talk about sports, and late at night it's got movies with a lot of tits and ass and stuff."

"No actual sex, though," mentioned Sorvig.

"No," Gail agreed. "Dickheads don't seem to fuck."

"That," said Beverly emphatically, "has not been my experience."

Everyone laughed except Beverly, who had confused herself by saying something unexpected and bitter. She waved at the television set suspended from the ceiling and said, "What the hey, let's watch the boob tube."

Maywell Hope shook his head. "Nothing on but trash."

"Listen," Jimmy Newton addressed Maywell, "if you're worried about what they'll say about the hurricane—"

"I'm not worried about it."

"—don't worry about it," Newton finished.

"I don't see the sense in worrying other people," said Maywell.

"What will be, will be," said Lester.

"Be quiet, Lester. Save it for one of your sermons."

"She's deflecting," Newton said.

"It's coming," Lester whispered, draining the last of his beer and raising a hand in holy testimony. *The Lord hurled a great wind upon the sea, and there was a mighty tempest on the sea.*

"Just what you want," muttered Gail, "when you're on vacation."

"Take me up and throw me into the sea!" shouted Lester. *"Then the sea will quiet down for you; for I know it is because of me that this great tempest has come upon you."*

"That's enough, now," cautioned Maywell.

"And the Lord appointed a great fish to swallow up Jonah; and Jonah was in the belly of the fish three days and three nights. But," said Lester, "that's aside the point."

"There is no storm coming, Lester."

"There is goddam *so,* Maywell Hope!" Lester protested, striking the bar top, making glasses bounce the length of it. "And if you had been on the island before, instead of larking off fornicating, you'd *know* that a storm is coming. Because you'd be able to feel it, like I feel it."

"You feel it, do you?"

"I feel it all around me, yes, sir. I feel the awesome power and fury of our Lord God. May I please have some rum?"

"The point is," said Jimmy Newton, "as far as I can tell, Claire's gonna miss this island. I could tell you more if I could get any of my damn phones to work. Hey! Do you have a two-way radio?"

"Aye." Maywell took a step backwards and opened some cupboard doors. "There you go."

Jimmy Newton stared with amazement. "What the fuck is that?"

"That's a radio," stated Maywell.

"Where'd you get it, from a museum?"

"That's a radio," Maywell insisted.

"Yeah, a fricking *crystal* radio. Jeez. We could listen to Ted Mack's *Amateur Hour* on that pile of shit."

"It works fine," said Maywell, flipping a toggle switch. The radio was moulded out of Bakelite. Glass tubes sprouted from it, each containing a tiny flower of thin wire. Maywell waited for a moment or two, but nothing happened. "Hold on," he remembered, and he reached underneath the bar and brought up the cardboard box that Lester had held cradled in his hands on the plane. Maywell took a knife and cut through the clear packing tape, pulled out some Styrofoam peanuts and tossed them away. He gingerly removed a tube and examined it closely, especially the socket end, where there was a rather complex arrangement of prongs. "It *will* work fine," he declared, "as soon as I put this in."

Beverly asked, "Mr. Hope, if you never believed the hurricane was coming, why did you send Lester to Florida to pick that up?"

By way of answer, Maywell raised his eyebrows and tilted his head ever so slightly toward Polly. She was just straightening up—she had joined Maywell behind the bar to sort through some invoices—and she caught him doing this. "Well," Polly announced, "nothing is more important than the comfort and safety of my guests. And that's what Maywell believes too. Isn't it, May?"

Hope nodded grimly.

Polly suddenly kissed him on the cheek. "Which is why," she said, "he's going to turn on the television now."

"All right, all right, we'll see what's what." Maywell picked up a blocky remote control, aimed it at the set and pressed the power button. Then he began to plow through the frequencies, the screen lighting with image and then collapsing into grey static between stations. There were flashes of baseball players, women in bathing suits, a man putting some small, furry animal into his mouth. "What was that?" wondered the girls.

Maywell Hope set the remote control aside when he saw a map of the Caribbean. A line cut across the screen. The line was solid on the right side, and in the middle was a little symbol $ showing that Hurricane Claire was currently well out at sea. A broken-lined projection of the storm's path extended from the symbol.

"What did I tell you?" said Jimmy Newton to Caldwell. "We ought to be in Cuba."

"Shit," said Beverly.

"What did *I* tell you?" demanded Maywell Hope. "You see that, Lester?"

"I see a map and some lines," Lester answered.

"Well, that's a relief," said Sorvig.

"Although there's still no guys around here," said Gail, and with that the girls polished off their drinks and said good night.

"Okay," said Jimmy Newton, climbing down from his bar stool. "I guess I'll go figure out how to get off of this damn island."

"I think you should just settle in, sir," Maywell called after him. "This island's hard to get off of at the best of times." He looked at Beverly and Caldwell. "You people must be disappointed."

Both shrugged, although for different reasons. Any larger action would have been too much for Beverly—her anger would overspill. Caldwell had no other reaction. His emotions were not available to him, in much the same manner as cable television is not available on the Galapagos Islands.

"But there's many delights to be had on Dampier Cay," Maywell continued, sounding like the chair of the chamber of commerce—which, as hard as it may be to believe, was a position he held. "For example, snorkelling. Or deep-sea fishing. But perhaps Dampier Cay's main claim to fame is its bonefish. Do either of you people fish?"

Caldwell nodded. "That's what I do."

"I used to fish with my grandfather," Beverly said. "That is, I spent hours sitting in a boat with him, threading pieces of worm onto the hook. Sometimes, though, when he got too drunk, I'd take over and fish."

"Dampier Cay happens to be home to the finest guide in the world. Not to mention the All-island Fly-fish Champion twelve out of twenty years." Maywell puffed out his bony chest to display the likeness on his T-shirt. "Bonefish Maywell, that's me."

"Well, then," said Caldwell, "let's do a little fishing."

"Yeah, let's," Beverly said.

"We'd have to leave early in the morning," warned Maywell. "High tide's at first light."

"I don't care what time we leave," said Caldwell. "It really makes no difference to me."

FOR SEVEN DAYS they had seen no twisters.

This was Beverly's first trip, although at the time she had expected it to be her last, her only. It had seemed like the end of a longer journey. First there were the two years spent in the land of the damned, which she viewed in some vague way as a holiday. But the truth finally dawned, this was no vacation, Beverly had never left the place; she'd been *born* in that land, was a certified damned citizen.

Near the end of the two years she'd got into difficulty with the law. She had been charged by the OPP with public nudity. It seemed an open-and-shut case, seeing as Beverly was arrested stark naked in Coronation Park. But the police report made no mention of the water surface, which she'd stumbled upon, coming home from God knows where. There was nothing in the report about how Lake Couchiching, that dawn, was as smooth as a mirror, or how the mist had formed into gently swirling towers on top of it. So Beverly had torn off her clothes and waded among the wind devils and waterspouts, and if that caused some concern to the members of the Orillia Road Runners, fifteen pudgy people out on their morning jog, well, Beverly really couldn't help that. The judge was lenient, and decreed that in lieu of a sentence or fine Beverly had to seek counselling. Beverly hated that. All of the professionals kept sticking their noses places they didn't belong.

Then she'd been arrested for destruction of public property and charged with vandalism. This was more serious—who would have thought stained glass windows cost so much?—but Beverly was able to mitigate the consequences by citing drink as the culprit. She proclaimed herself an alcoholic and promised to attend AA meetings. She went often, but she had no real trouble giving up liquor, because the stuff simply didn't work. Booze couldn't do what she needed done. Beverly didn't know what that was, exactly, so she took all the governors off her impulses, just to see where they took her.

She found herself prowling the streets on stormy nights.

And she became a physical sensation junkie, roaming around southern Ontario in search of fairs and midways, spending hundreds of dollars on the rides.

There came a day when the two interests met. She was in the town of Stayner on a hot summer day, sitting on the top of the Ferris wheel while the carnies down below loaded and unloaded customers. Suddenly the wind picked up, rocking the baskets on the antiquated contraption. The fairground echoed with screams. Dust flew in all directions, obscuring the world. Candy wrappers and cotton candy cones floated about. There came a force—cyclonic action—and things began to move around and around and around.

Then there was dead calm. It had been nothing, really, just a little blow, nothing the locals hadn't seen before. But Beverly had spotted the quarry.

She realized that she couldn't leave things up to chance, especially given her luck. As her grandfather said, Beverly was Jesus jinxed. (Sometimes, when her grandfather could get his hands on some money, he would take the bus to the racetrack in Barrie and wager on the trotters. He would leave Beverly alone in the apartment when he did this, even when she was five, six years old, fearful that she'd queer his luck. Even so, when he returned, drunk and penniless, he would blame her. *Jesus jinxed.*) Then one day, in the *Packet & Times,* she read a little filler piece about a company that took people to find tornadoes. *Bingo,* Beverly thought. She made a phone call and was dismayed to discover how much the endeavour would cost: a few thousand for the tour itself, not to mention transportation to Norman, Oklahoma. Her salary from Waubeshene Insurance alone would never get her there, so Beverly went back to Pilmer's Grocery and asked if she could once again have a job as an assistant cashier. Mr. Pilmer was a little reluctant, given her recent notoriety, but he finally agreed.

It was some months before she could afford to book her seat with the Tornado Hunter Company. The time wasn't wasted, however. Beverly was pleased to discover that southern Ontario is actually a wonderful place to live if one is interested in violent weather. She got pretty good at reading signs, both scientific data and omens presented in the sky. She read a lot of books about weather.

That was when she'd learned about Galveston.

But there were no organized tours in southern Ontario, not like in the Tornado Alley that slices through several middle American states. Beverly was also eager to go with the Tornado Hunter Company because they engaged the services of Jimmy Newton. She didn't own a computer back then, but she sometimes used the library's, and so had become a fan of Mr. Weather.

She was a little disappointed to discover when she arrived that there were two minivans and that she'd been assigned the one piloted by the young Larry DeWitt. Jimmy Newton drove the lead truck; Larry followed behind, drinking too much coffee and smoking cigarettes.

Jimmy Newton put them on supercells easily enough. They spent a lot of time staring at huge dark monuments to energy. The cells mushroomed toward heaven and spat lightning. The sight was awesome, but not what Beverly had come for. She realized that, despite her great interest, she was not really a weather weenie. She couldn't appreciate the mammati, no matter how well defined, and she wasn't satisfied with horizontal vort tubes.

Although she knew it was foolish, she blamed Larry for the failure to find actual tornadoes. She didn't blame Jimmy Newton, because Newton shared her disdain for displays of unfocused energy, no matter how grand. Newton would march toward the dark system in the sky, his little fists buckled onto his hips like he was some kind of matador, trying to madden cyclones, to infuriate them to the point where the wind devils would split from the mother and charge. When nothing was forthcoming, he would spin around, his nose stuck up and testing the air. He'd say something like, "Let's get on down to Ogallala. There's something forming up down there." Larry would still be staring at the supercell slack-jawed, his eyes clouded over with awe. Beverly would sometimes have to pull him away. "Mr. Newton says we should try near Ogallala," she'd say, and Larry DeWitt would blink and spend a second remembering who Beverly was, and why he was standing in the middle of some farmer's field in Nebraska.

So she blamed Larry for not finding the quarry; not only that, she found him dull—well, he *was* dull, Jimmy Newton called him Larry the Wit with dripping sarcasm—and only reasonably good-looking. Beverly was much more drawn to another man on the trip, a professor of medieval literature, who had long flaxen hair and a scar across one cheek. Although she never asked how he got it, it thrilled her to imagine that he'd taken part in swordplay arguing over some delicate point of academia. And this man seemed to be attracted to her; at nights he would seek her out in the lounge of the hotel/motel, and he would drink whisky while Beverly sipped Cokes. But nothing ever happened. The man was, at fundament, shy, almost removed from the human race. Most drinkers were. And also, Beverly eventually relaxed enough with him to tell him her story, and from then on all he saw when he looked at her was a walking wound.

On the seventh day, the last of the tour, they caught a twister. Funnily enough, the scene had not looked promising. They stood on the edge of a field and stared at a distant dark sky, and no one in the group held out much hope—except Jimmy Newton. Newton popped up and down, he waved his little arms with impatience that bordered on fury, and as she watched, the air on the earth's edge began to move, she could see it turning. The motion was visible because dust and dry straw and the like had been sucked into it, but Beverly preferred to ignore that fact. In her memory it was as if she watched the air turn hard and furious, watched it spin and blacken and touch down.

That's what Jimmy Newton said—"touch down"— although it was not quite that way. The twister had not exactly lighted upon the earth; the earth had risen to meet it. A belly of dust lifted gently and joined the darkening coil of wind. Then the tornado was alive, black and dancing and heading straight for the brace of minivans.

The other weather tourists were busy filming, armed with sleek compact digital recorders, except for the professor of medieval literature. He had a huge reflex camera mounted on an elaborate tripod, but he had time only to depress the button once before he had to start dismantling.

Beverly stared at the cyclone, barely noticing the commotion all around her. She heard Jimmy Newton cautioning people to get back into the van, but it meant nothing to her. Larry came up beside her and took her hand. But he didn't pull her away, instead he walked with her as she took a few small steps toward the tornado. Larry said, "Let's go, Bev," and then she broke, throwing his hand away and running as fast as she could toward the thing. Larry tackled her, and she fell face forward onto the ground, tasting dirt and feeling little fingers of wind tousling her hair. It almost had her, but Larry turned out to be stronger than she had imagined. He picked her up and carried her to the minivan, despite the fact that she thrashed and punched and snarled, pitching more manic a tantrum than Margaret ever had. The other chasers had to hold her down in the back seat, they had to physically subdue her. Larry muttered, "Shit shit oh shit," as he drove away, and if the tornado hadn't suddenly veered off, they all probably would have died.

That evening she had gone to Larry's motel room, surprised him while he was in the shower. He came to the door with a towel wrapped around his bony hips, suds still plugging his ears. Beverly was wet too, because the storm that had spawned the tornado still raged. Thunder crashed and lightning lit the world like garish Vegas neon.

She stepped into the room and pulled the towel away, pushing Larry back toward the bed. Larry figured this was his reward for saving her life, but he had it ass backwards. Larry had screwed things up, and Beverly was giving him a shot at some kind of redemption.

Their sex was passionate, at least at the beginning, Beverly and Larry the Wit clawing at each other, covering each other with fierce kisses. When he was inside her, Beverly asked if he knew about Galveston.

Larry was moving his hips with a certain rhythm, but it was no rhythm that meant anything to Beverly, as it communicated neither need nor pleasure.

"Do you know about Galveston?" she repeated, because Larry had made no response.

"I want to fuck you," he answered.

Beverly dug her fingers into his butt, which provoked a stuttering spasm that felt good to her for a moment, but she had clawed his ass with a certain anger. After all, she reflected, he *was* fucking her. What Larry the Wit meant was, *I'd like to fuck you without interruption or distraction.*

Beverly's adventure with the Tornado Hunter hadn't

completed any journey. When she whispered once again, "Do you know about Galveston?" all Larry did was grunt.

She began to weep.

"Yes, I do," answered Caldwell, sitting up on his little cot, turning toward the voice and finding a wall. "I know all about it." Sometimes images, imaginings, thoughts of Galveston, came to him with the force of memory—or what he remembered memory felt like.

He stood up then, stared into the darkness and waited for his eyes to adjust. He went into the washroom to urinate and was surprised to find that his penis was stiff, at least stiffer than usual. He had no erection—hadn't had one for a long, long time—but his penis was stiff enough that Caldwell wondered what stuff had been in his dreams. He took hold of his penis experimentally and pulled at it. There was actually a little stirring, the distant murmur of physical pleasure.

"I know all about Galveston," Caldwell whispered.

Once (Caldwell wasn't sure how long ago this was, perhaps it was even recently) he had summoned a call girl to his hotel room. The dispatcher had asked him a number of questions, trying to determine his predilections.

"Blonde or brunette?" asked the dispatcher.

"It doesn't really matter. Blonde," he decided, afraid that a girl with darker hair might favour Jaime.

"Right. Do you like full-bodied girls?" The dispatcher's voice had been ruined by cigarettes and her sentences were punctuated by greedy inhalations.

"I don't care. Just a girl. But she has to hurry."

"Oh, well, dear, it may be a little while. There's a big storm on the way."

"She has to hurry," Caldwell repeated. "She has to get here before the storm hits."

The dispatcher interpreted this as concern on Caldwell's part. "Well, all right." There was a long silence then; Caldwell imagined that the woman was consulting a clipboard or something. "Listen, sweetie, I can get Hester there in about twenty minutes, but I've got to tell you, she is dark-haired. And she's not to everybody's taste."

"Send Hester." Caldwell had pulled back the curtain and was staring at the sky. If he'd been asked, at that moment, where he was, he would have had only the weakest notion—the earth was flat and seemingly endless, he was in either the Canadian or American prairie—but he knew the sky intimately, he'd been watching the sky all afternoon. He had watched the clouds form, towering to the troposphere and then flattening out to form huge anvils. He had watched them darken, he'd watched them turn black. Now they shone with an eerie green tinge. There wasn't much time. Send this girl, this Hester.

But the weather arrived before the girl did. Caldwell saw it march down the main street of the town, catching pedestrians unawares. Hats were snapped off of heads, bags ripped out of hands. People rushed into doorways, they huddled under awnings. The storm gleefully went in after them, tearing away green canvas and pelting people with hailstones the size of golf balls.

Caldwell watched one woman who refused to take cover. She leant into the wind and made slow, halting headway. The wind sucked the dress almost off her body. There was not much to this dress, and what there was, was soaking wet. Caldwell could see the shape of her breasts, the dark nipples. He could see that she was wearing tiny panties. Caldwell realized this was Hester, because she'd trained her eyes on the hotel and wouldn't tear them away.

The storm pushed her over, knocking her to the sidewalk. She managed to get up on one knee and then she waited for a hole in the howling. When it came, she sprang up and ran. She disappeared from Caldwell's sight and then, perhaps five minutes later, there came a weak knocking at the hotel-room door.

When he opened it, the woman reeled in, giddy and befuddled. "Holy shit," she declared. "That's a fucker. That is a storm of Biblical proportions."

Caldwell saw why the dispatcher had said Hester was "not to everybody's taste." Her features were oddly assorted; her nose was too big, her eyes were too small, and her mouth was twisted by a scar that slashed across both lips. This scar made many of Hester's words sound strange, causing the "s" to whistle and the "f" to come with too much air.

Caldwell went to the little mini-bar, opened it up and offered this woman a drink.

"Oh, sure, yeah, whatever," she said, staring down at herself, trying to determine the damage done. Her knee was bloody, her dress soaked and her dark hair glued all over her back and shoulders. "Listen, bud, I'm a bit of a fucking mess here." She went to the washroom to get cleaned up and she didn't close the door behind her. "My father," she called out above the sound of a blow-dryer, "is a religious freak. A deeply religious freak. And according to him, storms are God's way of showing He's pissed. Like God is pissed. You know. Demonstrating His wrath. And walking over here, I'm thinking, hey, maybe, like, what am I, I'm a whore, so there's this big storm because God's ticked. But if He's mad at me, why is He taking it out on everybody else?"

"Ah," said Caldwell. "Good question." He sat on the bed, looking into a mirror that showed him the interior of the bathroom. Hester had a towel wrapped around her waist, her arms raised and her hands in motion, one wielding the dryer, one pulling at her hair. "In the Middle Ages," Caldwell said, "people thought that lightning was a sign that God was angry."

"Right. Only makes sense."

"So the whole deal was to try to appease God. Every church had a bell tower, you know, and they would send someone up to ring the bell. To try to make God happy. Of course, that was the worst place to be during a thunderstorm. Those bell-ringers would get killed all the time. But they kept doing it. For centuries." Caldwell often felt that he had been a bell-ringer in some other life, maybe even in this one.

Hester came to stand in front of Caldwell and let the towel drop to the ground. "Anything in particular you like, bud?"

When he said nothing, she took his hand and moved it first across her breasts, then over her belly, and finally put it between her soft thighs and held it there.

Caldwell looked out the window. The storm had gone, leaving behind only grey skies and a dull, steady rain. There was no energy left.

"Bud? You with me here?"

The rain had made everything indistinct. The buildings melted into the street, the street melted into the ground.

Hester sat down beside Caldwell and reached over and touched his penis through his trousers. "Come on, bud," she whispered, "let's get with the program." She unzipped him, snaked her hand through, caressed his cock softly. "Um . . ." Hester hesitated, then asked a question gently. "Do we have some sort of problem with the hydraulics here?"

"I'm sorry," Caldwell managed.

"Oh, hey, don't worry about it. Do you want me to try mouth-to-mouth resuscitation?"

"I don't think that would work," said Caldwell.

"There's drugs, you know, that you can take . . ."

"I know."

"Well, it's your call, buddy. You placed the order, you got to pay. Tell me what you want and we'll get to it."

"Can I tell you a story?"

"Hot damn," said Hester. "You hear about these freaks— no offence—who just want to talk, but I never got one before. So hell yes, bud, tell me a story."

Caldwell licked his lips and wondered where to begin. "One morning I got up," he said. "It was Saturday, and I had the house to myself, so I spread the paper out all over the kitchen table."

———

When he tells the story to Hester, Caldwell avoids speaking of the hour he spent waiting for Darla Featherstone. His wife and son had left the house to collect his mother and would meet him at the lottery office, where an oversized cheque would be issued and photographs taken. Caldwell went upstairs to the bedroom and threw himself down on the mattress, practising for the life of leisure that was to be his. He stretched out, rubbed his stomach contentedly, and noticed, almost by accident, that he had an erection and wondered idly what, if anything, he should do about it. Darla Featherstone had said that it might be a little while before she arrived, so Caldwell supposed he had at least five or ten minutes to spare. He reminded himself that he and Jaime would probably be making love later that evening (Jaime's favoured response to good news), but he was on the fence as to whether or not masturbation would help or hinder his evening's performance. Mind you, toying with his cock had kind of exacerbated the situation; he was now possessed of what Jaime called, with affection, a "snarler."

So he began to pull on it, and in his mind's eye he saw (not that he'd summoned her, more that she'd walked in of her own accord) Darla Featherstone. She was dancing as though she were a girl at Mystery's. She wore a sequined two-piece bikini, but she pulled it off almost immediately. In Caldwell's mind, Darla Featherstone turned around to do this. Her buttocks were flawless, and then, as she unhooked the top, she turned back and Caldwell could see her breasts, which, since there is no gravity in dreams, pointed heavenward.

Caldwell rushed to shove his wife Jaime onto that imaginary stage, because he felt guilty about whacking off to the phantom of Darla Featherstone, guilty that he'd dreamt Darla's body with the naive enthusiasm of his hormone-riddled students. He knew that her body could never be so perfect; in real life Darla would be pocked and puckered like everyone else. Jaime seemed to be making this point; she stood beside Darla and gave her a series of withering glances. Jaime's body was claimed by earthly forces. What had been nothing but muscle when she was twenty-one and provincial intercollegiate individual medley champ was now partly tallow. Still, he loved his wife's body, Caldwell did, and he pulled on his cock with all the enthusiasm he could muster. But when Caldwell came, Darla Featherstone was the only woman he saw.

He opened his eyes. He could see the world outside through the bedroom window. Ice pellets crackled against the glass, which was framed with rime. *That probably explains,* he thought, *what's keeping the people from the television station . . .*

There came a knock on the door and Caldwell threw himself off the bed, and was startled to find none of the things he expected—no nightstands, no brightly burnished bureau adorned with the three hockey trophies that Jaime grudgingly, laughingly, allowed him to keep in their bedroom. Instead, Caldwell saw two beds and an old washbasin, dimly lit by a weakly cracking dawn. Outside the sliding glass door stood Beverly, her arms wrapped around herself as protection against the night's chill. Caldwell slid the door open hesitantly.

"Hey," said Beverly, "did we come here to fish or to fool around?"

🌴🌴🌴

Maywell's boat was long and white, with a platform erected over the large outboard motor. There was no place for them to sit except beside Maywell on a small bench behind the steering console. The rest of the boat was taken up by fishing rods, rope and a long, thick pole carved at the top into a nasty point.

They travelled fast and they travelled far, that's how it seemed to Beverly. When she fished with her grandfather, the journey to the fishing spot was always undertaken at a much slower pace. Granddad would stop at the marina to gas up, then disappear into the building and leave Beverly sitting in the boat while a teenaged boy filled up the orange tank. Her grandfather would emerge perhaps half an hour later, a little wobbly on his legs, filled with optimism concerning the day's catch. He had almost always forgotten to purchase worms, which was his avowed purpose in entering the marina proper. He would light a cigarette and send Beverly back in.

Maywell piloted his boat in grim silence, again something Beverly's grandfather never did. Grandfather would sing, tell filthy jokes, reminisce about his childhood. Beverly would experience this all again, years later, when she joined him in the land of the damned, sitting in the Dominion Tap Room day after day after grey day. She was sometimes startled out of her stupor to realize that she knew the ending of a story. What was startling was the smallness of her grandfather's life, the fact that he had but a handful of old, musty stories and no prospect of acquiring new ones.

Caldwell was remembering journeys to fishing grounds too, trips with Andy sitting in the bow, turned around to face the open water. Andy always wore a ridiculous hat, something that a Foreign Legionnaire might don, with a long visor and a hank of material dangling down in the back to guard his neck from sunburn. He wore the hat in emulation of his "hero," at least his fishing hero, who through the media of an eponymous magazine and a weekly television show had managed to fill the boy's head with odd and complex ideas. Accordingly, Andy identified Lake Simcoe as "mesotrophic" and wanted to fish places where no fish had ever been caught. Caldwell pointed out that he had long lived beside the lake, learned its secrets from various uncles and friends, but Andy would not be swayed. He would identify some aspect of the lakeside—a tiny weed-choked bay—and demand that they put in. Caldwell would argue that there were no fish in there, never had been, and fishlessness might break his son's heart. Actually, truth be told, Andy would enjoy the fishing whether he caught anything or not, allegiance to his heroes being more important to him than results. It was Caldwell's heart that would sustain damage, back in the days when it was whole, his son's slightest aches ripping through his soul second-hand.

An ugly ridge of red, porous rock shot out of the water; behind it lay a mangrove swamp. Maywell pulled back on the throttle, making the boat *whoa* abruptly. As the boat kicked back and forth, Maywell pushed at a toggle. There was a light whirring noise, which Caldwell identified as the automatic tilt. Then Maywell bolted forward, picking up the long pole. When he returned, he stepped over Beverly and nimbly took his position atop the platform. He poled gently into the mangroves, peering into the shallow water.

"Ever fished for bone before?" he demanded.

"Yep," said Caldwell.

"Nope," said Beverly.

"The fish come into the flats to feed. They come in with the tide, which we're on right now, so we should be able to find us some. They're hard to see. If they're moving toward us, you might see a shadow move. If they're lying aslant, you'll see nothing. They're like a mirror from the side, invisible."

"Well," marvelled Beverly, "isn't that clever of them?"

Maywell looked down from his platform, his face set. "No, it isn't clever of them, ma'am," he answered lowly. "That's just nature."

"Nature is clever."

"Nature is neither clever nor dull, ma'am," said Maywell. "Nature is simply what is."

Now Beverly turned to Caldwell. "What's your opinion?"

"Oh, nature is clever enough," said Caldwell, taking up the fishing rod. "Just not as clever as it thinks it is." He stepped up onto the bow, his legs bent slightly for balance. He pulled the line out of the reel in a few quick, short motions, dumping it in coils near his feet. Caldwell swung around briefly, checking for clearance on his back cast, picked up the flyline and laid it out in front of the boat. As he stripped back in, he spoke to Maywell without looking at him. "Just tell me what to do, Cap'n."

Maywell propelled the boat noiselessly forward with the long pole. He turned his head mechanically back and forth, searching, then snapped almost to attention. "Bonefish, sir."

Caldwell turned slightly to his right. The rubber on the sole of his shoe gave off a small squeak as it pivoted on the whitewashed wood.

"No, they're gone now," intoned Maywell. "You've spooked them."

"What?" demanded Caldwell in a hoarse whisper.

"You've got to be quiet, sir," said Maywell. "They're skittish creatures."

Caldwell had been fishing with guides before, he knew that Maywell's deferential "sir" really substituted for something more disdainful.

"It seems to me that all creatures are skittish," announced Beverly.

"Quite so, ma'am." Maywell put the pole in the crook of his arm, fumbled with a matchbook, lit up yet another cigarette. "They tend to be. Bonefish, sir."

Caldwell tensed and turned himself, keeping his treacherous feet planted firmly atop the wood. "Where?" he whispered.

"Two o'clock. Fifty feet away, sir."

Caldwell squinted through dark lenses and saw nothing.

"They're gone, sir. You waited too long."

"There's a bonefish, Mr. Caldwell," said Beverly.

Caldwell squinted. "Where?"

"Three, um," she said, considering accuracy, "*twenty.*"

This time Caldwell turned and saw the shadows.

"There's three of them, sir," announced Maywell.

Caldwell picked up the line and threw it back and forth a few times.

"No, sir, they're gone. Too much false-casting."

Caldwell felt a little bubble of anger rise up within him, a bubble that popped and dissipated long before it hit the surface. He stepped down from the casting platform and held out the rod to Beverly. "You give it a try."

She accepted the rod and almost vaulted up to the bow. She peeled line from the reel, laying it neatly beside her, and then she assumed a slight crouch, peering into the world.

"Have you ever fly-fished before, ma'am?" asked Maywell quietly.

"I have not."

"It's not as simple as it looks," said Maywell.

"Nothing is." She stiffened. "Bonefish, sir."

"Where?" asked Maywell.

"Three forty-seven." Beverly lifted the rod suddenly, throwing the line into the back of the boat. The line snaked along the bottom—Caldwell had to step to one side to allow it passage—and then was in the air. Beverly snapped the line back and forth, rushing her back cast and making a big belly, but she managed a fairly tidy lay-down. The fly began to sink, and even as Maywell said, "Oh, yes, ma'am, I see them . . ." the line went taut. Then the air was filled with a high-pitched *whir* as the fish flew toward the edge of the world.

"Keep your rod-tip up, ma'am."

"My rod-tip *is* up."

"Yes, ma'am."

Her grandfather used to say that—"Keep your rod-tip up." Late in the fishing day, around four-thirty or five o'clock, it was one of the few sentences he could manage. By that time he would have consumed a bottle of rye, and be crumpled in the bottom of the boat, his head up on one thwart, his feet crossed over one another. He would estimate his day's catch as inadequate. He believed, quite wrongly, that he was considered the finest perch fisherman in Orillia. He'd won the annual derby one year, fluking across some anomalous holding area, and although decades had passed, he believed he was being judged against that mark each time he went angling. So he would make Beverly fish with two rods, one on either side of the boat, and when she hooked a fish, he would growl, "Keep your rod-tip up."

Maywell repeated, "Keep your rod-tip up," and Beverly succumbed to a temptation she'd felt first at nine or ten years of age. She tossed the fishing rod into the water and yelled, "Run!" She chuckled, because, after all, it was fairly humorous to tell a fish to *run,* but then she quieted because she'd just done something very odd, something that would keep her visiting the professionals.

The men in the boat didn't seem to think she was insane, exactly. Caldwell only laughed, not very loudly but deeply, giving out a bark that buckled his body for a brief moment. Maywell's reaction was much more emphatic. He leapt down from the poling platform into the water. While doing this, he managed to drop his pole into the boat, and then, picking his legs up high, he ran after the rod that was being dragged away by the hooked fish. He did all this without comment, without expression, as though this was something fishing guides had to do regularly—retrieve rods thrown into the water by women who were still angry with their alcoholic grandfathers.

Maywell dove forward and wrapped his hand around the corked butt of the fly rod, and managed to get himself into a kneeling position, lifting the rod out of the water and leaning back, trying to find tension, a connection to the fish. But the top half of the fly rod had worked itself out of the ferrule, and the pole collapsed. Maywell grabbed the line above the joint, twisting his wrist so that he had it firmly, and then struggled to stand upright. He reached forward and took the line from beyond the tip, then brought his other hand forward to join it, abandoning the useless fly rod altogether. He had hold of the running line, and he circled his hands like a prizefighter working the speed bag, gathering monofilament, and in a few moments he grunted and his arms jerked and he was tight to the fish.

The bonefish splashed the surface about a hundred yards away. Maywell spit out his cigarette and began to pull. He raised his arms to his chest and then furiously cocked and circled them, taking up line. The skein around his fingers got tighter and tighter; red began to leak out from around it, blood from where the monofilament had worked itself into Maywell's leathery skin.

"Let it go," advised Caldwell.

"I think not, sir," muttered Maywell.

As she watched Maywell—with undeniable admiration—Beverly noted that shadows moved across his body, that his figure would be darkened and then suddenly illuminated. She looked up at the sky and saw that it was studded with little clouds, that these clouds moved quickly overhead. She looked at the mangroves, saw how the breeze was ruffling them.

"The wind has changed," Beverly said, and although she spoke very quietly, Maywell heard. For a moment he forgot his fight, lifted his face to the sun and noted the movement of clouds. But then the fish splashed, perhaps fifty feet away, turned and started another run, and Maywell's hands were yanked away from him, and the effort of pulling the line back squeezed drops of blood that darkened the water around his legs.

Maywell placed the flyline between his teeth and shook the monofilament from his hands. He began to gather in the thicker stuff. Soon the bonefish splashed twenty feet away. Maywell marched sideways, pulling the fish with him, up onto a small sandbar. He yanked and tugged, pulled and hoisted, and then he quickly ran his left hand into the water. He missed on his first attempt, but on the second he managed to take hold of the creature's belly. He lifted the bonefish up into the air; the silver side reflected so much sun that the creature seemed to be made out of light. Maywell gently worked the fly out of the fish's maw.

"Please let it go," said Beverly. "I don't want to eat it."

Maywell was struggling to regain his breath, no easy feat given all the cigarettes he smoked. He began to cough, and it was many long moments before he could speak a sentence. "One doesn't eat bonefish, ma'am." Maywell lowered the fish back into the water and let it go. Then he splashed over to the boat and climbed wearily into it. He turned on the motor and announced, "That's enough fishing for today."

As the boat neared the Water's Edge, Caldwell could see Jimmy Newton standing on the grounds in front of the main building, his hands on his hips, his chin lifted with smug defiance. Caldwell recognized the stance as the one George Reeves adopted during the opening credits to the old television show *Superman*. Caldwell spotted Lester too. He had a canvas sack slung over his back and was scurrying from little plant to little plant.

Maywell slowed up at the last possible instant, throwing a wake that splashed against the pylons, wetting even the sign that demanded *NO WAKE*. It hardly mattered; there were no other boats moored there. When they left, there'd been three anchored in the little harbour, a sport-fishing craft and two big cruisers, but they'd fled, hurrying off to find better shelter. This place was wide open, Caldwell saw. The other side of the island was more hostile, but this shore was hardly safe haven.

The points that formed the harbour were rounded and held only a few bent palm trees.

Maywell leapt up on the dock and threw the painter around a cleat. He marched across the dirt road and up toward the main building.

Lester knelt beside a small stripling and drove a thin stick into the ground beside it. He removed from his canvas sack a little plastic twist-tie and deftly attached the stalk to the stick, wiping his hands with evident satisfaction.

"Lester," said Maywell, "what are you doing?"

"*Strengthen ye the weak hands,*" intoned Lester, "*and confirm the feeble knees.*"

Caldwell got out of the boat, turning back to Beverly and extending his hand. She smiled up at him but didn't accept his help, preferring to grab the whitewashed ladder and pull herself up. They walked together toward the Water's Edge.

"You saw the television," said Maywell to Lester. "The hurricane's going to miss us."

Newton—nodding happily at Beverly and Caldwell as they passed—spoke without turning toward Maywell. "You'd better turn the set back on, pal."

Maywell turned on him. "What do you mean?"

"I mean that the world, the globe, is a great big pinball machine, man, and Claire just got smacked by a bumper. Big trough of cold air sitting up there. An anomaly. *Chaos.* And the storm smacked it, bounced off, and she's coming back. And, oh yeah, she's got English on her now, *baby.*"

Maywell looked again at the man kneeling by the pitiful stripling. "Stop it, Lester," he said.

Lester stood up suddenly and bolted, but he only went about twelve feet, to where another young plant was being stirred by the breeze. He knelt down and began work with his stick and twist-tie. "The eighty-third sam," he intoned. "'Oh, my God, make them like a wheel. As the stubble before the wind. As the fire burneth a wood, and as the flame setteth the mountains on fire, so persecute them with thy tempest, and make them afraid with thy storm.'"

Maywell waved a hand at Lester dismissively and then levelled his sunglasses at Jimmy Newton. "So now they're saying the storm may hit us?"

"Yeah, they're saying she *may*," said Newton. "I'm saying she *will*."

Maywell lit another cigarette, pulled a piece of tobacco from a lip that was bloodless and caked with dead skin. "Another couple of hours," he said, "they'll be saying something else again."

"Look at that," said Beverly, pointing across the island to the eastern sky, to the shadow at the edge of the world.

They all turned to look. The horizon was smudged with a thick black line, and the darkness shimmied and pulsated into the welkin.

"What will be, will be," whispered Lester, "and it looks like it's going to be soon."

"Can't be the storm." Jimmy Newton shook his head.

"I think I know what it is," said Maywell Hope.

Caldwell realized what it was too, understanding why the shadow changed shape, why it pulsed and quivered. But as he was about to say, Beverly held up a finger. "Shhh. Listen."

They could hear the sound the shadow made, like a thousand violin bows quivering across the top of the world.

"Ah-yuh," said Maywell. "I've read about this in the book."

As the shadow drew near, it began to splinter, as did the sound, exploding into a huge chord. The air was rippled by a host of rhythms. There was screeching and cawing and wails made piercing by separation.

Birds covered the sky.

Beverly managed to whisper, "Isn't it beautiful?" and took Caldwell's hand in her own.

The others could not speak for a long moment, then Jimmy Newton said, "Shit. I've seen birds come before a storm before, but never anything like this."

"'The sky was darkned,'" began Maywell.

"Darkned?" wondered Jimmy.

"'And all manner of Bird appeared in every parcel of the sky.'"

"Where's that from?" asked Beverly, but Maywell was walking briskly away.

"I've got work to do," he said.

"So now," Jimmy Newton called after him, "you believe the hurricane is coming?"

"Oh, she's coming," agreed Maywell Hope. "People lie or are mistaken or believe what they want. But *birds* . . ." Maywell spun around and waved a hand irritably. "Come along, Lester."

BEVERLY TRIED THE FIRST PART OF HER STORY out on Caldwell over coffee, sitting at the long bar in the Pirate's Lair. She was worried that he might be frightened away, but the advent of the storm made her giddy and reckless. Still, she didn't launch right into it.

"I enjoyed fishing with you today, Mr. Caldwell."

Caldwell nodded. He didn't supply his first name, nor did he echo the compliment. Apparently he was going to converse with a woman. They were going to share information, interesting tidbits and pieces of personal history. The prospect unnerved him.

"The only fishing I've ever done," said Beverly, "was on Lake Simcoe, with my grandfather."

Caldwell opened his mouth and a small sound came out. Beverly interpreted it as polite response, an interjection of encouraging interest, so she continued before anything could stop her. "I was brought up by my grandfather. My parents died when I was a baby."

Really what Caldwell had almost said was, *Hey, I used to fish on Simcoe too. I fished there with my dad and my uncle Basil and then I fished there with my son, Andy.* But he hadn't said it, and now Beverly was telling him the story of how her parents died.

She began with an evocation of her mother, Brenda. This was based on nothing, really, beyond her grandfather's drunken assertions that Beverly favoured her mother, that in his soggy mind the two seemed like sisters. Beverly made Brenda dreamy and poetic, which is what Beverly would have been like if not for the forsaken nature of her life. "My mother was a very spiritual young girl," Beverly said. "She was attracted to mysteries."

And her father was nothing if not a mystery. Beverly's grandfather rarely spoke of Gerald, except when he should have been passed out in the Dominion Tap Room but for some reason was still talking. So when Beverly told the story to Caldwell, she elaborated on the few facts she had. Her father was born in England, for instance, that much she knew, so in her telling Gerald acquired vaguely royal blood. He was certainly aristocratic at least; he had no job or profession, nor had he need of one. Gerald had money enough for his needs, which were few but expensive: he needed money for cigarettes, thousands of them, he needed money for liquor, vast quantities of it, and he needed money for heroin.

Beverly formed her impression of her father from various sources. She remembered a photograph of Gerald. He wore a T-shirt, thick spectacles, and he smoked a cigarette; even in faded black and white the nicotine stains were evident on both hands.

She had seen this photograph fairly recently, in the office of one of her counsellors, who had determined that the story of Gerald and her mother lay at the root of Beverly's so-called problems. This counsellor—the very aggressive Dr. Noth— had produced the old Toronto *Telegram* suddenly, in the middle of a dull session. Apparently Dr. Noth thought this might spark Beverly into animated conversation, although Beverly was a very long way from that. She was perpetually tranked, for one thing, which was Dr. Noth's doing, so why the fat, nasty woman thought this photograph might rev her up was anybody's guess.

Beverly gazed at the photograph and her mind idly threw up questions. Where had the newspaper got it? Why wasn't her mother in it? Beverly recognized the background as Orillia; indeed, Gerald was standing in Coronation Park, the water bright behind him. Beverly imagined that he was never far away from Brenda while he was in Canada, and then it dawned on her that her mother had taken the photograph, and in that instant Beverly felt connection. She handed the newspaper back to Dr. Noth—the counsellor's nostrils were flaring with anticipation—and said, "Motherfucker sure smoked a lot."

Beverly knew about the liquor because she had it in her blood: the black Celtic thirst. True, she could have inherited the curse from her grandfather, but it seemed so strong in Beverly that she couldn't credit more than a generation's distance from the source.

She knew about the heroin because everyone in town knew about the heroin and spoke of it often, hoping that it would explain what had taken place. "Of course," people would say, "he was a heroin addict." No one in Orillia really knew anything about heroin, so they'd embellish the story with sentences like, "Mind you, he'd snorted a bunch of heroin." Beverly imagined, maybe remembered, how it truly was, how Gerald would spend what seemed like hours methodically preparing the drug in a spoon at the gas stove, how he would disinfect the syringe (Beverly imagined, maybe remembered, that he'd had a laughable fear of germs) and adroitly drive the needle into his arm.

Beverly paused in her telling; Caldwell looked confused. "You keep saying, 'I imagine, maybe remember,'" he pointed out.

"Right, I do keep saying that." She took a sip of coffee, allowing herself a moment to consider her behaviour objectively, to see if she had crossed once again into creepy oddness. She decided she was on fairly firm ground here. "Memory is an interesting thing."

Caldwell said, "I don't really have one," before he could stop himself.

"Beg your pardon?"

"I don't really have a memory. Not one like other people have one. Not a memory that goes, you know, from back then until now. I have *memories*, but I have trouble putting them in order."

"What order are you trying to put them in?"

"Just order. 'This happened, then this happened, this happened next.'"

"Chronological? Or, um, *causal*? This happened *because* that happened."

Caldwell avoided the question. "But what do you mean, 'I imagine, maybe remember?'"

"I *saw* these things," Beverly answered. "I know I saw my father doing heroin. I must have. It was only a one-room apartment, so I must have watched him, I must have seen him. But I was not even two years old when it happened."

Beverly sat in a high chair in the corner of the apartment. She had a large bowl of soup and a wooden spoon. They gave her a wooden spoon because she was an active baby, who liked to smash and pound things. She had once cut her mouth with a metal spoon, that's how frantic she was to feed herself, so they took that one away from her and gave her this wooden one.

As to what they were arguing about, Beverly had no idea. She was not even two years old. All young couples—Brenda was only nineteen, Gerald twenty-five—argue. Over money. Perhaps they argued over Gerald's drug habit, but Beverly had a hunch they didn't. They lived in a world where drug habits were commonplace, where it took a brave beast indeed to wander around without a crutch. Most people drank in the land of the damned, but the adventurous found the good drugs. So Brenda likely stood in the corner, watching, picking up the wooden spoon when Beverly spat it across the floor.

Perhaps they didn't even fight. People presuppose a room full of violence, but this doesn't necessarily hold. Ennui, world-weariness, can be as destructive as rage.

Gail and Sorvig came in, wet from a swim in the ocean. They were still determined to have fun, although their brows were furrowed with worry. Jimmy Newton followed after. Confident that the hurricane was on its way, he had decided to relax and enjoy himself. He was wearing only swim trunks, and the sun had already reddened his belly and shoulders. Jimmy had spread zinc ointment down his nose and across his brow.

"What I don't get," said Sorvig, "is this: if this huge hurricane is coming, why is it so beautiful outside?"

"Ah! Good question!" said Mr. Weather eagerly. It was just like Jimmy to think that the girls might be impressed with his weather-related pedantics. "It's because of the outflow. You see, the force of the storm essentially blows all other weather away. So for a while yet there's going to be nothing but blue skies. But that's what it is—nothing. No weather."

"Well," said Gail, "at least we get to work on our tans before we get killed."

Beverly imagines, maybe remembers, quiet. She hears peaceful music. There was an old record player in the apartment, and Gerald had a huge and eclectic collection of LPs and 45s. He usually listened to blues and plaintive country and western, but for this occasion he pulled out one of his classical albums, Ravel's *Pavane for a Dead Princess*. This is what Beverly hears, anyway. Just the music, just the jeremiad. Beverly hears no screaming as Gerald slices Brenda's throat, as he carves into her body. Beverly bangs with her wooden spoon. Gerald then kills himself, with the knife. This is the part that people find most disturbing—not the evisceration of the young bride, rather the fact that Gerald was able to take his own life in the same manner: first opening his throat and then his stomach.

Beverly looked into Caldwell's eyes. She wasn't searching for understanding, because she knew none of this explained anything, or was itself explainable. It all just set the weird and messy stage. Beverly was looking for some sort of acceptance, maybe, acknowledgment that life is full of black holes. Perhaps what she was looking for was *no* reaction. A sincere lack of interest in her past would be a great act of kindness.

What Caldwell did was ask an unrelated question, almost as though he hadn't been listening. "What did you mean back there at the airport, when you said 'I've done what you just did?'"

"I've used the past—the pain—to get what I wanted," she said. "And what's funny is, most people would think, you know, *How heartless. How little it must mean.* They don't understand. When you get to that point, where you can *use* it like that, you're way past suffering, mere suffering. You're . . ." Beverly searched for the right word.

"Removed," suggested Caldwell.

"Right."

"And what do you think it would take," wondered Caldwell, "to get unremoved?"

"Well, that's easy, Mr. Caldwell," Beverly answered. "It would take an act of God."

POLLY WAS IN THE BATHTUB, because that was part of her routine. Between eleven a.m. and noon, Polly sat in the bathtub. Not always for the entire hour, mind you, although that happened on occasion. The bath was part of her routine, and Polly wasn't about to change that because of nasty weather being on its way.

In the quarters Polly kept (two large rooms snugged behind the reception desk in the main building, connected by a short, narrow washroom) there was a deep old tub, the stands fashioned to resemble lion's legs. Polly had a plastic tray that hooked onto the rim and stretched from one side to the other. It was loaded with bills, invoices, personal correspondence, newspapers, whatever paperback book she happened to be reading at the time. She could get quite a lot of clerical work done, fill in a few squares of a crossword, and it was the only chance she ever got to read. Polly enjoyed mystery novels—green-spined Penguins were her favourite—although they were hard to come by on Dampier Cay. There was no bookshop on the island; the local general store, Millroy's, kept a few titles, but only best-sellers, thrillers centred around serial killers and the most grisly of crimes. And even these books went unsold, turning dusty and brittle. The natives simply didn't seem to think much of reading as a pastime. Take her lover, Maywell, as an example: the man owned exactly one book.

Maywell entered the bathroom, pausing to look at her. Polly's feet were pointing toward him, one crossed over the other on the lip of the tub. She wriggled her toes by way of greeting, because she had a pencil in one hand and newspaper in the other. She was trying to think of a five-letter word for "three-toed animal," but she abandoned that for a moment and watched Maywell as he looked at her. It always occurred to her at such moments that Maywell was like an artist, a painter judging a canvas-in-progress. His gaze was cold and steadfast, sweeping the length of her body, searching for imperfection but receptive to beauty.

He grunted, continued past the tub. Polly heard the toilet seat being flipped up and then the heavy cascade. "Oh, May," she muttered.

"I have to go," he protested. "And you won't let me piss outside."

"I don't like you to pee where all the guests can see you," she returned.

"Lester and I are going into Williamsville."

"What for?"

"The storm's coming."

"Mm-hmm?"

"We need supplies."

"We have supplies," said Polly, filling in the word *tapir*. "Remember? I got you to buy water, gasoline, batteries, flashlights . . ."

"Uh-yuh." Maywell was finally through. "There's still a few supplies we need."

"I see."

"Never know with this sort of thing."

"Too true." Polly knew pretty well what supplies Maywell was referring to, but she decided not to press the point. It was his life, after all. She put aside the pencil and puzzle and lay back in the tub. "Just remember, there's work to be done around here. We have to board up the windows . . ."

"Yes'm."

"Secure everything, clear away potential debris."

"Yes'm."

She loved the way Maywell said "yes, ma'am," deferential and insolent at the same time. "You know what?" she said. "I'm feeling a little bit frisky."

Maywell cocked an eyebrow.

"Must be something in the air," she said. "Doesn't the atmosphere get all charged up before a storm?"

"Could do," replied Maywell.

"It's kind of exciting, isn't it? I mean, I guess it's scary, but at the same time, I don't know . . . perhaps a little taste of mortality whets the appetite for—"

Maywell appeared by the side of the tub, pushed the tub rack down to the far end, bent over and took hold of her. He lifted her from the water, took her into the next room and set her down on the bed.

Lester waited for Maywell in the Pirate's Lair, trying to think of useful things to do. He went behind the bar and plucked up the radio tube, the one he'd been sent to fetch from Miami. A memory came of the night he'd spent there, and Lester winced with shame. He had gone to a club where women paraded around naked, which might be pleasant enough but was no way for a preacher-man to behave. Lester counted that as one of his main professions—he was a gardener, a psalmist and a preacher.

He wasn't ordained, mind you, but the people of Dampier Cay didn't mind. The islanders were actually skeptical of church-sanctioned ministers, preferring gospellers who were not constrained by orthodoxy. Lester preached with the blissed-out enthusiasm of a jazz musician, his eyes disappearing beneath the lids as he searched out heaven. His sermons, delivered out of doors, most often on the big rocks overlooking the ocean, were very popular. People were willing to forgive him his excesses, and he had a few, although nowhere near as many as when he was young. They used to think of Lester as bad news, particularly when he was in the company of the come-to-naught Maywell Hope.

Lester opened the radio cupboard and spent a few moments looking at the thing. He plugged in the new tube, flicked the toggle switch to make sure everything was working. Then he closed the cupboard doors again. That wasn't the sort of chore he was supposed to do; clean work was Maywell's lookout. Except that Maywell was no good with anything that used electrical power, so Lester often did little things and then made no mention of it. Maywell would find the radio in working order and allow Miss Polly and everyone else to believe that he'd done it himself. Which was fair enough, really, just one of the rewards Maywell had earned by finding his way into Miss Polly's bed.

Sometimes Lester had to laugh, thinking how well Maywell had done with his life. He used to be the scrawny little white boy whom no one liked, the latest in a succession of unpopular Hope men. Hope men were violent, lazy and given to strong drink. The Hope genealogy was bizarre, too. On the endpapers of Lester's bible was his own family tree, and Lester often marvelled at all the branches. He liked to follow them and discover (it always felt like a discovery) that he was related to Sherman Vaughan, who had left the island fourteen years ago and now played the trumpet with B.B. King. Or Marcella Knight, who was the most beautiful woman on the island—although that was actually a disappointment, because Lester would have liked to have had a taste of Marcella, and there was an inviolable rule against relations with anybody whose name appeared in the fly-leaf of the family bible. The point being, Maywell's bible—not that he or any other Hope ever owned one—would not have contained any such complicated design. The Hope lineage proceeded father to son, always just the single boy, seemingly with no woman involved. Like a jellyfish might divide into two, although it seemed to Lester like he met some fellow in a tavern who told him that wasn't so, about jellyfish.

Maywell Hope finally appeared in the Pirate's Lair, tugging the baseball cap down, fixing sunglasses over his eyes. He nodded at Lester and left the building. Lester hurried behind, and didn't catch up until they were halfway down the little rise.

"Did you tell Miss Polly we were going to town?" Lester asked innocently, although he knew he was being prankish—how long does it take to tell a woman you're going to town?—and Maywell knew it too.

Maywell let it go, this time. Sometimes he'd let things go, sometimes he'd get all righteous and start throwing punches. There was a time when Lester would have hit back, indeed there was a time when Lester could have kicked Maywell's scrawny white butt. But all that was different, now that Maywell had found his way into Polly's bed. Now Lester was forced to trot after Maywell like a dog. Maywell did the clean work, Lester was the one with shit all over his hands.

They climbed into the rusted minivan. Lester sat in the passenger's seat. When there were guests being driven around, of course, Lester was expected to crawl into one of the rear seats. But now it was just the two of them, which—his complicated emotions notwithstanding—made Lester enormously happy.

Maywell cranked the key and the vehicle yowled into ignition. He threw the thing into gear (not *first* gear, Lester noticed; Maywell was a piss-poor driver) and piloted out onto the gravel road. Lester rested his arm out the window and settled back into his seat, pretending, for a few minutes, that he and Maywell were still best friends. "We got things to do in town," he announced for no reason.

"We have plenty to do at the Edge, getting ready for the storm," Maywell said. "So I don't want you going into the Royal."

"No, sir, I won't do that." Although Lester *would* do it, fuck Maywell Hope. He'd do whatever the hell he wanted to. He turned and looked out to sea. Far to the east, beyond the horizon, the sky was darkening.

Maywell stopped the car in front of Millroy's General Store. Lester threw open his door and scampered away, making a beeline for the New Royal Tavern. "Be back in half an hour!" Maywell called after him.

"Yes, sir!" Lester returned, although it was all a show. For whose benefit, Maywell couldn't say, but it was all a show, both his own bossiness and Lester's servility. He understood Lester's bitterness; Lester resented the fact that Maywell shared Polly's bed and was accorded certain privileges and other favours. What Lester didn't appreciate was the fact that Maywell loved Polly. Mind you, Lester didn't exactly *know* that, because it was Maywell's great secret. He kept his love secret because he suspected it was imperfect. What else could one expect from the Last of the Merry Boys?

Upton Belshaw stopped Maywell, pressing a hand against his chest, outside Millroy's. Upton removed his hat and nodded a few times before speaking. "They're making this storm out to be fierce," he finally said.

Maywell nodded. "There's going to be some wind and rain, Upton. Make sure your windows are boarded."

"Now there's the thing, Maywell. The front window broke and I haven't replaced it. Should I put board up anyway?"

"I would, Upton."

"Ah."

"Don't worry. There'll be a big blow and then there won't."

"I'm a little concerned that my house . . . I don't believe my house is up to it. I have young children, Maywell."

"I know that, Upton."

"I was wondering if we could come over to the Water's Edge."

Maywell pictured the Water's Edge, the main building

sitting atop the little rise. "If I were you, Upton, I'd take my family to the big hotel."

Then he walked into the store. The shelves were almost empty. They were never overstocked at the best of times, but now there were but a couple of boxes of cereal, a few tin cans, and that was that. Maywell went to the counter. June gazed at him steadily, and Maywell detected a slight hint of fear in the whites of her eyes.

"Carton of Sweet Caps," he said, pulling bills out of his pocket, smoothing them out in his hands.

June shook her head, very slightly. "No cartons left."

"I'll take whatever packs you got."

"We're out of Sweet Caporals," June almost whispered.

"Rothmans, then."

"No. I'm sorry."

"Winstons. Silk Cut. Senior Service."

"We don't have any cigarettes, Maywell."

Maywell made a careful inspection, turning his head slowly as though scanning the flats for bonefish. He saw lottery tickets, a few video cassettes, some empty pop bottles that had been returned for the deposit. "None?"

"People have been stocking up. We were supposed to get some more today, but the flight was cancelled."

"June, you knew I'd need smokes."

"Maywell, you told me you were going to quit. You said that was the last carton you were ever going to buy."

"Oh, for Christ's sake, June, I say that every goddam time, don't I?"

"I'm sorry, Maywell."

"You're absolutely sure that there's none, not a solitary pack, in the store? Don't you want to check the back room or anything?"

"Maywell . . . we are out of cigarettes."

Maywell entered the New Royal Tavern, which was pretty grandly named considering that the bar proper was banged together out of plywood and the appurtenances amounted to two posters, both years out of date, team photographs of the Tottenham Hotspurs. There were a few stools scattered about, two of them currently occupied. Johnny Reyes was sitting in a corner, and Lester had claimed a seat beside the bar so that he could rest an elbow there and balance his head on his folded knuckles. When Maywell entered the establishment, Lester downed his shot of rum and then tapped the countertop for another. Kirby moved slowly behind the bar, drawing up a big bottle of Captain Morgan's from down below, filling a shot glass and overturning this into Lester's empty tumbler. Then Kirby filled the shot glass again and pushed the thing toward Maywell.

"You know I won't drink that," said Maywell.

"I just thought," returned Kirby, "that you'd be sick of white milk by now."

Lester laughed, too loudly. "Kirby got you good, Maywell. *Sick of white milk.* You should kick his ass."

Maywell understood that he had been the topic of conversation in the bar for the past little while. He looked over at Johnny Reyes, who was nodding slowly, staring down at his own feet. "Sick of white milk," Johnny repeated. "Maywell ought to be sick of white milk."

"Milk's good for you," noted Maywell. "You need milk to grow. Come along, Lester."

"I believe I'll just have another drink."

"We have work to do."

"That woman got you doing *work*?" demanded Kirby. "Fuck, May. She must have one goddam glory hole."

"That'll be enough of that, Kirby. Don't you have business to attend to? Seems to me there's a storm headed our way."

Johnny Reyes looked up from the close inspection of his feet, the rubber flip-flops and burnished calluses. "Hey, Maywell," he muttered, so quietly that the words barely made it to Hope's ears, "are you thinking of sticking around for this one?"

Maywell Hope had been off Dampier Cay only twice in his lifetime. He knew that many people would account that as odd. His knowledge of the world was therefore limited, informed largely by television-watching, although he did that only rarely. There were nights, as Maywell tended bar in the Pirate's Lair, that the guests had no questions for him, nights when everyone just sipped cocktails in a relatively civilized and subdued manner, and Maywell, growing bored, would turn on the television set. He would watch CNN and listen to tales of chaos. He had seldom heard of the countries the reporters talked about. He had grown up in Williamsville, and it had only been twenty-odd years since some representative of the British government had stopped by to establish mandatory education. Before that, schooling was more or less optional— and not even a viable option for Maywell, burdened as he was by the Hope family name.

Maywell's concept of the globe was based in large part on his reading, and rereading, of William Dampier's *A New Voyage Round the World*. So in Maywell's mind there was the *Atlantick Sea*, and Dampier Cay was in the *Caribee*. He thought of the largest island to the southwest as *Hispaniola*, although he was grudgingly aware that it had at some time been divided into Haiti and the Dominican Republic. Hope knew his unique reference points made him an object of curiosity. His fishing clients often grilled him about the immediate geography; Maywell might refer to *New Andalusia*, which would earn him a look of confusion, then as much laughter as the clients thought they could get away with.

What the clients didn't know about were the wondrous things that were included in Maywell's world view from reading *A New Voyage Round the World*. Penguin-Fruit, for instance, which *are wholsome, and never offend the Stomach; but those that eat many, will find a heat or tickling in their Fundament*. That book was filled with such goings-on as would make the CNN reporters tremble and quake: *Therefore Captain Swan immediately march'd out of the Town, and his Men all followed him; and when he came to the place where the Engagement had been, he saw all his Men that went out in the Morning lying dead. They were stript, and so cut and mangled, that he scarce knew one Man.*

Maywell Hope had read this book since he was a child. Indeed, it had been read to him as an infant, as he lay awaiting sleep. The book was one of three his father owned, the other two being thick tomes dealing with navigation. Maywell's father, Marlon, was barely literate, and this book, filled with whimsical spelling, seemed to forgive that fault. Marlon, like Hope men for generations, also suspected that there might be some clue as to his genealogy somewhere in its pages. There was no privateer named Hope in the book, but perhaps the original progenitor had changed it, or the name had been changed somewhere along the line. Perhaps Marlon and Maywell (and Maxwell and Melvale Hope, and all the others) were descended from Dampier's right-hand man, Basil Ringrose. Or perhaps they were descended from the Chirurgeon, Mr. Wafer, the mischievous fellow who was always getting into difficulties: *Our Chirurgeon, Mr. Wafer, came to a sad disaster here: being drying his Powder, a careless Fellow passed by with his Pipe lighted, and set fire to his Powder, which blew up and scorched his Knee* . . . Mind you, the greater mystery was the identity of the Hope family's Eve. If there was a woman sailing with the Merry Boys, William Dampier writes nothing about it.

Maywell's favourite story in the book—at least, one he had read many times, particularly over the last few years—proceeded like this: Dampier and the Merry Boys, sailing the *Batchelor's Delight,* found themselves set upon by a huge storm. They put into a cove and anchored there, furling all the sails because the wind would have torn them to tatters. The ship weathered well until the winds began to shift. Because of the furious counter-clockwise motion of hurricanes, the winds howl first toward the west and then, after the passing of the eye, in the opposite direction. Dampier had to turn the ship but knew that he couldn't unfurl any sails in order to do so. So he instructed all of the Merry Boys to ascend the forward rigging and cling to the foreshrouds. Maywell had imagined these men, high in the air, clutching the screaming ropes, and each other, their bodies offering enough resistance to the wind to finally turn the ship about.

Maywell wished that he could have been there.

Because Maywell had been off the island only twice in his life. He had gone once to Cuba and once to Jamaica, both trips undertaken to find women, since he had had the women on Dampier Cay, all those who were willing to have *him*. On both occasions when he'd been away from home, Dampier Cay was hit by storms. The first was not too serious; it had taken out a few homes in Williamsville and destroyed some of the yachts in the Government Harbour. The second time he'd been away, Fred had come to call. Seventeen dead on Dampier Cay, including Lester's boy, Powell. Maywell returned home to find that many things had simply disappeared. Even the Royal Tavern was nowhere to be seen, although its place was marked by a dead refrigerator, lying on its side, wide open.

CALDWELL AND BEVERLY sat in the Pirate's Lair and waited for the storm. Both seemed calm, but Caldwell's patience was that of a fisherman—who is willing only to wait one more moment, over and over again—and Beverly was busy holding her emotions hostage. This is what she'd learned from the professionals, how to ride shotgun on the weird stuff.

Jimmy Newton came in with Gail and Sorvig. The girls still wore their bathing suits, but Jimmy had put on some sort of safari gear, a khaki jacket and shorts. All of the pockets were jammed with stuff: light meters, lens cleaners, cords to connect his electronic gear. Two pockets held small still cameras, there was a large thirty-five-millimetre slung around his neck, and in a pouch over his crotch he had the beauty, his newest toy, a digital minicam that was guaranteed to give him broadcast-ready quality.

"See, *me*," said Gail, "I'm just trying to go through life clean, you know what I mean? If I can avoid, you know, terminal illness, um, psychopathic boyfriends and, well, *hurricanes* . . ."

"Yeah," said Jimmy, but he was shaking his head. "Except they're different. They're different kinds of problems. There's human stuff and then there's, I don't know . . ."

"God stuff?" suggested Sorvig.

"Weather *is* God," said Jimmy Newton. "God is weather. The natives, the cavemen, they saw, you know, the sky all lit up with lightning, they heard thunder, they said, 'Hell yes, there's someone up there and He's pissed.' So, yeah, it's kind of God stuff, but it's . . . the thing is, it's just a lot bigger than human stuff. Okay, Gail, you say you're trying to go through life clean. But here's the thing. Let's say that you, um, got cancer, and HIV, and, um, your boyfriend attacks you twice a week with a machete. That and any other shit you care to imagine. Take *that* outside when a category three is passing through. That's clean, baby. That's all your problems blown away."

"I don't think I agree with you, Mr. Newton," said Beverly. "I think God *is* the little human problems. All that other stuff is flash and filigree, you know. A cheap trick. *Pay no attention to the man behind the curtain.*"

"Well, you're entitled to your opinion, but you are just a little nuts."

"Perhaps. But I know what I'm talking about. You may not remember me, but I went on a tornado-hunting expedition with you."

"Yeah, I remember. You're a friend of Larry DeWitt's."

"Well, we had sex once, but that hardly makes us friends."

"Right."

"But what struck me about the tornado—when we finally found one, thanks to you, Mr. Newton—was that it was composed mostly of the, um, *detritus* of human lives. Condoms, candy wrappers. Nails and wedding rings."

Caldwell opened his mouth to say, "I know what you mean," but he choked on the first word and reached instead for his whisky.

"Hey," said Jimmy, throwing open the trap and walking behind the bar, "I wonder if they fixed this piece of crap yet." He opened the cupboard doors, exposing the old Bakelite radio. He reached out, flipped the toggle switch, and the silver filaments in the tubes began to glow. Jimmy unclipped a small microphone from the side of the machine, a silver disc that filled the palm of his hand, and depressed a button on the side. "Come in, come in." He was answered by an intense spurt of static. "Hmm," he scowled, working a dial, trying to locate a serviceable frequency.

"Hello?" came a broken voice. "Who's this?"

"This?" responded Jimmy Newton. "This is Mister fricking Weather. Who's *this*?"

"This is Burt Gilchrist. My wife and I came to look after the property in case the hurricane hits," explained the voice. "But we're thinking we made a mistake. I mean, what can we do? What can we do when the storm comes?"

"Well, you should know the procedure, Gilchrist. You bought property in the hot zone."

"Who *is* this?" shouted Burt Gilchrist, and in the background his wife could be heard asking, "Who is it?"

"Over and out," said Newton, spinning the dial, squinting to watch a needle pass over a grid. "NOAA. Come in, NOAA." As he waited for an answer, Jimmy cocked his wrist to the side and toyed idly with the microphone, flipping it up and down. After a moment he tried again, returning the metal disc to his lips and thumbing the button. "NOAA," he said. "Come in, NOAA. This is Newton on Dampier Cay."

A voice returned suddenly. "Newton? You're on Dampier Cay?"

Jimmy Newton grinned widely and looked at his companions, vastly proud of himself. He spoke into the microphone. "Yeppers. I'm on Dampier Cay."

"Well—it's been good knowing you."

"Aha!" shouted Newton gleefully. "So she's big?"

"Jimmy, go to a safe band," said the voice on the radio. "Go to eighty-seven."

Newton twisted the dial. The radio screamed and made little electronic burping sounds. A voice came: "You there, Jimmy?"

"Yeah."

"Well, you bought it this time, son. Claire has sucked up Daphne. She's heading due west at twenty knots, but we think she's going to pick up speed any time. And we can't see how anything's going to change her mind, so you know . . . if there's anything like high country on Dampier Cay, you better get there."

"I'm about as high as she gets. Maybe twenty-five feet."

"That might not be good enough, Jimmy."

"Right," said Jimmy Newton. "Is she going to make four?"

The man on the radio didn't respond right away. "At least four, Newton."

"Thank you, NOAA. Over and out."

Beverly thought about Noah.

She knew that Newton had been saying "NOAA"—the acronym stood for the National Oceanic and Atmospheric Administration—but in her thoughts the forecaster was Noah. He stood on the deck of the ark. He furrowed his brow and stared at the sky, and predicted that the rains would last for forty days and forty nights. Noah's sons, clutching crooked staves, herded animals onto the ark. The animals came in pairs, as everyone knows, and in Beverly's mind they boarded as couples, bound by love and devotion. Quadrupeds moved in comfortable unison, their heads touching. Some of the birds were actually mating as they came. The more exotic birds were belly to belly, while pigeons and seagulls did it doggy-style, flapping their wings with arrhythmic ecstasy.

Then Beverly imagined all the damned and dying creatures. Water covered the face of the earth, and the air was filled with frantic whinnies, howls and ululations. As water flowed through valleys and around mountains, eddies were formed, whirlpools that dragged the animals down. All of their eyes were white, emptied by panic.

She told Caldwell the second part of her story.

Margaret's swimming was simply not improving, and even though Steve told her over and over again not to worry, Beverly couldn't help herself. She told her daughter that she'd have to practise more. Beverly checked the schedule the young people at the Y had given her. There was a free swim Saturdays at two o'clock.

Beverly drove Margaret down to the YMCA. The little girl pushed buttons on the little radio in the dashboard until she at last heard the song that was number one, the song that the most people liked. She sat back in her seat and sang along tunelessly, then stopped singing abruptly as a troubled thought crept across her face. "Did you bring my swim cap?"

"No," Beverly snapped. "That is not my responsibility. I make sure your suit and towel are clean and dry. You are supposed to remember to bring your bathing cap, nose plugs, soap and shampoo."

"I forgot it."

"Well, then, you will have to go without one."

Margaret scowled. "The chlorine is bad for my hair."

"I know it is. That is why you're supposed to bring a bathing cap."

Margaret's hair was her pride and joy. Truth to tell, it was Beverly's pride and joy. It was long, falling all the way to the little girl's waist, and golden, full of curves and curls that caught sunlight. Margaret took good care of her hair; this confusion over the swim cap was just that, confusion—it didn't reflect neglect on anyone's part.

(Caldwell reached over and took both of Beverly's hands from where they lay, like wounded creatures, on her lap. Both of her small hands fit into one of his own.)

There was a lounge area at the YMCA in Orillia, a few round tables and stools. Off to one side an old woman with milky eyes sold sandwiches, apples and coffee. On the other side was a curved glass wall, and through this parents could watch their kids in the pool. Beverly sat at one of the little tables with a stack of books. Before they left, she wanted to acquire at least elementary Spanish, as well as something of the history of the country.

From time to time she glanced up and looked through the glass wall. The pool was crowded, as though all of the children in town had decided at the same time to go swimming. The kids were behaving badly, as kids will. They ran on the slick decks, they cannonballed into the shallow end, where signs demanded they not jump at all.

Where, exactly, was the supervision? Beverly wasn't the only one wondering that, because those words were spoken aloud by another mother sitting nearby. There were two lifeguards on duty, a boy and girl, not yet out of their teens. The boy strolled about the deck with a paddleboard grasped behind his back. The girl sat atop the small tower with her legs crossed and her hands folded. She should have been hunched forward, peering downwards with hawklike intensity—her supervisor should have demanded it of her.

Steve sat in an office tucked into the corner, and every few minutes he would pop his head out. Sometimes he'd take a walk around the perimeter. He wore track pants, a sweatshirt and thick-soled running shoes, all emblematic of his *don't worry* attitude, because if for any reason he needed to leap into the pool, this apparel would hamper his rescue efforts. Indeed, this point was brought up at the coroner's inquest, although no one really paid much attention to it; Steve had comported himself in a valiant manner, even Beverly conceded that.

Beverly tried to pretend that what she saw through the glass wall was normal, and maybe it was. She would later find out—sitting at the coroner's inquest, staring down at her toes because she could not abide the scrutiny of the artists from the newspapers—that another guard had called in sick that day.

Anyway, even if there had been a full contingent of guards, even if they'd been absolutely focused on the activity in the pool, it is still likely that tragedy would have occurred.

Because, as Steve pointed out at the inquest, attention is paid to the middle depths of the pool, which is where souls are lost. People at the sides of the pool are usually safe, and that is why no one noticed little Margaret clinging there. No one noticed that her head was a foot below the surface, that she had been there for a few minutes. No one knew that her hair, her long hair, had been sucked into one of the filtration system's intake pipes.

Steve saw her first, blew the whistle and hollered, clearing the pool. He leapt in, and his efforts to save Margaret were furious but useless. He could not pry Beverly's daughter away from the wall.

At the coroner's inquest a physicist from the university explained why. It had to do with the vortex created by the water rushing through the intake pipe.

It had to do with cyclonic action.

Beverly and Caldwell walked outside, where the wind might dry her tears. It was a warm wind, and still very gentle at this point.

They walked along the gravel road, past cottages "J" and "K," and stopped outside the churchyard. They stared at the little graveyard. The stones were ancient, their faces obscured by lichen and moss. There were crosses there, whitewashed barnboard nailed together at right angles. Most of the names were washed away by time, although some could still be read: *Angela, Age Two; Naomi; Marvelle, No Years Old*. There were no flowers in the graveyard; if there ever had been any, the wind had blown them away.

"There was a guy I read about," said Caldwell, who could not take his eyes away from a crude marker that read *Andrew*, "who bought a barometer."

"Mm-hmm?"

"And he took it home and took it out of the box and it read really low, I don't know how low . . ."

"Well," said Beverly, "the record low at sea level is twenty-five point six nine."

"Oh," nodded Caldwell. "So it wasn't that low, probably, maybe it was twenty-eight or something, the point is, he thought he'd got a dud, you know, so he drove into town to the post office to send it back to the manufacturer, and when he got—"

—back, his house was gone, thought Beverly.

"—back, his house was gone."

"Really?"

"Wiped out by a hurricane."

"It was probably the freak hurricane of 1938, which caught the northeastern United States by complete surprise."

"I think it probably was. Five hundred dead in that one."

"Closer to six."

Caldwell nodded. He imagined that the six hundred lost souls divided up this way: two hundred children, two hundred wives, two hundred husbands who'd just happened not to be at home. They were off running errands, checking on faulty barometers and things like that.

Caldwell told the rest of his story to Beverly.

When she arrived, Darla Featherstone placed her fingertips on Caldwell's chest. It was a suggestive, sexual touch, at least, so it seemed to Caldwell in the moment he had to savour it. Behind Darla stood a cameraman; he hunkered over and squinted into the eyepiece of his machine. A red light flashed above the lens. Caldwell understood that he was being filmed, so he grinned and winked. The cameraman was protected by an elaborate plastic umbrella that attached somehow to his shoulders. This was covered with snow, pebbled and crusted with ice.

Caldwell opened the door wider, not understanding why Darla and the cameraman remained outside. Darla Featherstone shivered, her bottom lip quivered. Caldwell put this all down to the cold, so he gestured toward the warm kitchen. And maybe it was the emptiness there behind him, or maybe it was something in Darla's face, but Caldwell knew before he heard the words spoken.

Darla Featherstone said, "There's been an accident."

"So she drove me out there," Caldwell said. "Darla Featherstone did. With the cameraman in the back seat. With his camera going, I think. I don't know. I never turned around or anything, but he was there in the back seat of this car with his camera. And I remember thinking, you know, is she driving me out there because, I don't know, she's a human being, or am I—am I *news*? And then I felt, you know, like shit, because I wasn't news. I wish I had been news. I should have been news. Jaime was news. Andy was news. My mother was news."

"I remember that storm," said Beverly. "I remember that Saturday. I drove Margaret to the Y for her swim lesson."

"This transport truck was going north on Highway 26—my mom's nursing home was out near there—and he must have been going, I don't know, *fast*, because he just sailed over the median and, um . . . *Squashed like a bug.* That's what the *Sun* newspaper said. The big headline. *Squashed like a bug.* Because we drove a VW. A Beetle."

Beverly remembered seeing that headline. She'd allowed herself to drift close enough to the red *Sun* box to see the front page displayed behind the plastic. She saw enough to understand the cryptic headline, and part of her thought it was clever. She hadn't purchased the newspaper or anything, she was hardly that ghoulish.

"The next day," Caldwell went on—he'd been dreading this day for years, when for some reason he no longer had problems with his memory—"the funeral director came over to the house, and he's showing me all these photographs of coffins, and I'm asking how much is this one, how much is that one, and then I remembered. I was rich. I'd just won the provincial lottery. Sixteen million dollars. So I just turned to the last page of his binder, you know, where there were these golden coffins. And I said, 'Three of these.'"

Lester appeared beside them. He too stood and stared at the little graveyard. He held a bottle of rum in his hands, and had a sip before speaking. "Mind out for Maywell," Lester said. "Something's put him in a piss-poor mood." He tried to hitch up his trousers then, fumbling with the bottle, splashing liquor down the front. "I got work to do. I have to chop off all the weak branches. From the bamboo and the monkey puzzle tree. The spiny branches from high up in the kapok. Mind you"— he had another sip, almost for rhetorical purposes—"that won't help any when the trees themselves come out of the ground." Lester pointed at a stone in the graveyard's corner. A tear rolled out of his eye. "The last storm came in the middle of the night. We never knew it was coming. Nobody said anything about it. I don't know if they knew and didn't tell us, or if they didn't know themselves. I know *they* didn't die."

The rain started then, warm and heavy. Lester turned his head upwards, so it could wash away his tears. He drained the bottle of rum and tossed it into the churchyard.

"Well," said Caldwell, "I'm sure we'll be all right."

Lester looked at him. "Is that really what you think? Or do you think that this island is going to get wiped off the face of the earth?"

Caldwell looked around and shrugged. "Well, Lester. What will be, will be."

Lester smiled gently. "You got that fucking right, sir." Then he lay down on the ground and fell asleep.

Beverly looked at Caldwell. "I think we should get him out of the rain," she said, pushing open the little gate. Caldwell bent over and took hold of the gardener's shoulders, and dragged him toward the pale blue church.

The door lacked a handle, and Caldwell backed through it easily, although the hinges still managed to send up an awful howl. There were no more than eight pews in the church, two sets of four across from each other, and before them a crude pulpit. Caldwell pulled Lester into the aisle and set him down there. Lester turned over on his side and slipped his hands, palms pressed together and fingers touching, underneath his head.

Beverly had followed them into the church, and although Caldwell noted her trepidation, he put it down to the fact that the church was dark inside, full of shadows. He did not know that Beverly had made no peace with God, that in fact she hated Him and expected retribution if He should ever get her in His sights.

Caldwell didn't hate God, mostly because he had never really loved Him. As a young man, he might have professed a belief in the Almighty's existence, and when he played sports he often joined pre-game prayer circles, linking hands with his fellow athletes and muttering small entreaties. But after the game, if his side had won, Caldwell would never offer up thanks like his Christian teammates. He would tear off his clothes and stand under the shower and exalt in his own strength. He had no need of God back then, and he was decent enough, in some strange way, not to blame God now.

Not Beverly.

She blamed God and made no secret of it. Indeed, she'd got into trouble for blaming God. There had been an incident, something the authorities might have been willing to overlook had it not come so closely upon the heels of her arrest for public indecency. In fact, the authorities *did* overlook it, in the sense that Beverly was not found guilty of the crime of vandalism, but she was ordered to attend additional counselling sessions and pay for the stained glass window.

The police report stated that she'd been hurling stones through the elaborate and years-old stained glass window at Our Lady of Perpetual Mercy. The window pictured the Virgin (strangely faceless, her features hidden by a cowl) cradling the Infant Jesus. Birds crowded the scene, hundreds of them, packed so tightly that the metal forming the bottom of one creature's wing often formed the top of another's.

The police report made no mention of the weather, the storm in heaven. (Just as the authorities had missed the fact that Beverly's naked presence in the shallow bay had nothing to do with nudity and everything to do with the columns of mist that twisted awkwardly toward the sky.) No one pointed out that when Beverly had been arrested, the sky was boiling with black cloud, lightning cracked across the roof of the

world, quivering strokes of blue light. Yet no rain or hail fell to
the ground, which struck Beverly as very, very strange. Mind
you, she was pretty drunk, having left the Dominion Tap Room
after hours of inebriated communion. Her grandfather lay in a
crumpled heap over by the church's garbage cans. He'd
crawled over there when he thought he was going to vomit,
which was as close as the old man came to thoughtfulness. He
hadn't, thanks in large part to the fact that he hadn't eaten anything for days; instead, he heaved a couple of dry retches and
then fell asleep.

Leaving Beverly to ponder the fact that nothing fell from
the sky. Forcing her to the conclusion that God can do nothing right. God must be a buffoon, He fucks everything up. It
was in a spirit of sarcastic helpfulness that Beverly picked up
a handful of stones and threw them toward Mary and Child
shining over her. She was surprised when the stones pierced
the glass. Then she recalled stories of mothers demonstrating
inhuman strength, of mothers lifting cars off of their children,
wrestling polar bears to the ground when they threatened their
infants. This was the same sort of thing. In a matter of minutes she had broken almost all of the panes.

"Maybe we should go back to the cottages," suggested Caldwell.

Beverly shook her head. "No. It's not time, yet." She leant
forward and, rising up on her toes, kissed Caldwell on the lips.
"Let's help get ready for the storm," she said. "Let's do all the
little human stuff first."

MAYWELL HOPE boarded up the windows, standing in the rain and longing for a smoke. This wasn't supposed to be his work, it was Lester's, but Maywell felt sorry for Lester in a vague way. Pity was an emotion that didn't really sit well in Maywell's heart, so on occasion he did Lester's chores for him. Lester was not much good at the chores anyway, sloppy at the best of times, especially so when he had a snootful. Not to mention the fact that Lester was nowhere to be found. Maywell also undertook the labour to fill his hands with wood and tools, because his hands looked very naked without a cigarette in them. He had nails in his mouth, too, big, long three-inchers that tasted bitterly of rust.

"You need any help with that?"

Maywell turned to find Caldwell there, wet from the rain but oddly happy. He wore a smile that Maywell hadn't seen before. Maywell spat nails into his hand so that he could speak. "You could put your shoulder up against the board, if you don't mind, sir."

Caldwell leant against the plywood. Maywell aimed a nail and began to hammer.

"Can I ask you a question, sir?"

"Shoot."

"Well, what is it with you people? You and the woman and Newton. You like storms. Why?"

"Oh." Caldwell pretended to be thinking about this, although it was the one thing he knew, a certainty that claimed his cold centre. "Energy."

"How's that?"

"Storms have energy."

"Uh-yeah."

"It's hard to explain."

"No." Maywell shook his head. "You've done it. Storms have energy. And I take it that you don't?"

Caldwell shrugged. "You see, something happened to me."

Hope drove another nail, sinking it with three well-aimed blows. "Something happens to a good number of us, sir," he commented. "And I wouldn't want to be one of the others."

Caldwell surprised himself by laughing at this. "You got a point there, Maywell."

"So you've found your storm, sir. You realize you may not walk away from this one?"

"Life and existence aren't the same thing," said Caldwell.

"There, you've lost me," said Maywell, picking up a sheet of plywood and walking toward another window.

Beverly helped Polly transport stuff into a storage area, a crawl space located beneath the Pirate's Lair, accessed by a trap door behind the bar. Polly stood waist-deep in the opening, her arms outstretched, while Beverly delivered cases of liquor, pots and pans. Polly stacked them in an orderly fashion.

"You and Mr. Caldwell," said Polly, "seem to be hitting it off."

"Hmmm." Beverly brushed hair out of her eyes and picked

up a case of beer. "Isn't that a funny expression, though? Hitting *what* off? Hitting something off *what?*"

Polly could not resist sounding, for a second, like a holiday brochure. "The balmy, sunny climate in the Caribbean is responsible for many a romance."

"Is that so?" Beverly seemed to receive this as new data to be processed. "Then just think what might happen when the storm hits."

Jimmy Newton carried much of his equipment up to the main building at the Water's Edge. He set his digital camera up in the dining room, mounting it atop a tripod; the camera was attached to his laptop, which sat on one of the tables; and the laptop was attached to a small metal tower, which Newton placed in what he calculated to be the exact middle of the room.

Then he sat at a table, his hands folded neatly on top, and smiled into the lens. "Hey," he said. "I'm here in Dampier Cay, which you guys have never heard of. I'm sitting in this place called the Water's Edge, and we're waiting for Hurricane Claire. She should make landfall in three, three and a half hours. There should still be a little light, so I'm going to try to get some footage, and hopefully all this new technological stuff will work and you guys should get it live. Oh," he added, reacting to a sound behind him, turning to look, "here come my buddies Gail and Sorvig. They aren't chasers, in fact they're a little pissed off . . . Hey, girls, come here, smile into the camera and say hello to the folks back home."

Gail and Sorvig sat down at the table and looked quizzically at the camera. They had finally abandoned their swimsuits, and were dressed in jeans and T-shirts. Both held brushes and were pulling them through their wet hair. "What is that, Jimbo?" asked Gail.

"*That,*" said Newton proudly, "is my groovy new digicam, and that over there is a GSM system, and with any luck at all we're going live on the World Wide Web."

"Live?" asked Sorvig.

"Yeah. Anybody you want to say hello to?"

"Yeah," said Gail. "We want to say hello to our boss, Andy Probert. Hey, asshole," she began, and Sorvig completed the thought, "You should have let us change weeks."

It was perhaps six o'clock in the afternoon when the first winds, the first forceful and malevolent winds, came to Dampier Cay, heralded by a fanfare of waves suddenly breaking against the rocks on the east side of the island with a sound like a cymbal crash. And then the strange humming started; everything that was not of the earth but merely attached to it began to moan. Wires sang, high-pitched and plaintive. Power lines chanted wearily.

Maywell Hope entered the pale blue church a little cautiously, like a drunk trying to steal into his own home in the middle of the night, afraid of shattering lamps and waking loved ones. He stood in the aisle between the pews for a moment, waiting for his eyes to adjust to the gloom. Like all Hope men, he had an odd relationship with the church. There was a sense in which he wasn't even *allowed* in the place, certainly not when there was any kind of religious ceremony taking place. When weddings occurred, Maywell was expected to wait outside. The islanders maintained a superstition that it was good luck to have Maywell Hope throw the first handful of rice, but he knew they were simply being kind, that his presence inside would have made people uncomfortable. Not because of anything he'd ever done, or his father or grandfather, but there had long been a darkness attached to the Hope name. He had been born godless—born with a pirate's heart—and everyone knew it. What they didn't know was that it was Maywell Hope who painted the church, every year, carefully applying a coat of pale blue to match the sky.

He took a few steps forward, knelt down and put a finger to Lester's shoulder. The gardener was instantly awake, bolting upright, scrambling to his feet, spinning around to confront Maywell, who waited for the troubled dreams to clear from Lester's eyes. "Come on up to the main house," he said.

Lester took a step forward and stumbled, still groggy with rum. Maywell put his arm around Lester's shoulder to steady him, and together they left the church.

🌴🌴🌴🌴

THEN THERE WAS NOTHING to do but wait.

They assembled in the Pirate's Lair, which was dark and dismal behind its wall of boarded-up windows. Weak illumination came from the television set in the corner, tuned to CNN. There was a reporter and a small camera crew on Dampier Cay, staying at the big hotel at the other end of the island. Every now and again—although not as often as the people in the Pirate's Lair might have hoped—CNN would cut to this coverage. The reporter, Seth Wallaby, stood on the grounds of the big hotel, the deserted pool behind him. He clutched a microphone in one hand; with the other he made sure that a small receiver stayed plugged into his ear. He was dressed in an old-fashioned manner, wearing a beige trench coat cinched by a wide belt. Its function was not so much to keep Seth Wallaby dry but rather to identify him as a journalist and to give some crude measure of the wind speed; the tails and lapels of the garment flapped and whirred audibly. Each time the network cut back to Seth Wallaby, the flapping was more excited.

The advent of Hurricane Claire was not the big news of the day. NOAA predicted that its path would take it across a few islands—Jamaica was preparing for it—and then Central America. It would lose some power as it stamped across the land, and re-intensify out over the water, but the meteorologists felt it would then turn northwest. It might threaten Belize and the Yucatán, and perhaps other parts of Mexico were in danger, but Claire posed no threat to the United States of America, so CNN slotted its coverage appropriately. There was other, better, news. It had recently been discovered that a congressman was sleeping with another congressman's daughter, and although she was of consenting age, the fact that one man was a Republican and the other a Democrat lent this item an enticing and salacious angle.

Each time Seth Wallaby appeared, Polly tsked with irritation and said, "He could have stayed here. And his cameraman, producer, whatever. I would have given them a good deal. Our rooms are nicer." This seemed a controvertible statement—the big hotel looked rather grand, with elegant wrought iron balconies—but no one saw fit to challenge her. Maywell would grunt each time she made the pronouncement, but it was a vague sound, and could have been either agreement or argument.

"Do you remember when Miller Fulbright's son was born?" he demanded of Polly.

"What?"

"Miller Fulbright. A few weeks ago. Had a baby girl. Named her Antoinette."

"Well, yeah, May, I remember, but I can't see—"

"He gave me a cigar."

"Uh-huh?"

"I put it somewhere behind the bar here."

"Right. It got all dry and crumbly. I threw it away."

"Uh."

"Sorry!"

"How long ago was this, you threw it away?"

Gail and Sorvig had set up a little boom box near the far end of the long room. They were working their way through a small pile of CDs, dancing with grim purpose.

Lester joined them from time to time. Surprisingly, he showed himself to be a fine dancer, although an idiosyncratic one. He bent at the waist and held his hands up high, and while his feet usually made small, deft steps, occasionally he would throw one high into the air. He would snap upright and fold backwards, his bosom aimed toward heaven, his pelvis gyrating.

The wind was howling so loudly outside the Water's Edge that the music from the machine was all but inaudible. Gail and Sorvig, Lester too, seemed to be dancing to the tempest, timing their big motions to the crescendos of the storm's roar.

Caldwell sat beside Beverly at the bar. He reached over to touch her, pressing his hand over hers.

Beverly smiled at Caldwell. "Do you know about Galveston?" she asked.

Caldwell nodded. "Yeah."

"Good."

A while later, the wind started finding its way into the building.

Not the big wind, the mother, but offshoots and tendrils. The pages on Polly's clipboard flapped and turned themselves. Potted plants leaned back, snapped upright; they lost leaves and petals, which floated in the air. The little winds pushed Beverly's hair across her face, hiding her eyes.

Then Claire began to demand entry into the main building, testing every nail that Maywell had driven. She tried to pry the boards away, making the wood scream as though tortured. When the nails held, Polly noted that fact aloud, saying, "Good job, May."

Jimmy Newton reminded her, "She's not here yet. The storm hasn't made landfall."

The radio cackled and a voice came into the Pirate's Lair. "This is Burt Gilchrist and his wife. Please. Somebody."

Maywell scowled at the radio and rubbed his face. He lifted down the microphone and twisted at controls, making the radio yawp and yelp. "Hello, Mr. Gilchrist," he said. "How goes it?"

"I was unfaithful," said Burt Gilchrist. "With Doris Blembecker. I confessed it to my wife."

Maywell looked at the other people in the Pirate's Lair, trying to judge who would best deal with the situation. After a long moment he hammered the button with his thumb and said, "It's good you made your peace, Mr. Gilchrist."

"She told me that she was unfaithful too."

"Well, what's sauce for the goose and all that."

"What does that *mean*?" demanded Burt Gilchrist.

"Now is not a time for anger," said Maywell. "Now is a time to tell your wife you love her."

"Because we might die?"

"We might."

"Is there a . . . do you have a priest there?"

"No, sir. We surely don't. Now, you've got to get off the radio, Mr. Gilchrist. We've got to keep the airwaves free."

"It was with Pete Carney. My *best friend*."

"Over and out, now," said Maywell Hope.

Thunder broke the air, an enormous rumble that shook everything. Gail and Sorvig fell into each other. Lester tumbled backwards onto his bony ass. Caldwell's whisky glass leapt away from his hand and shattered.

Jimmy Newton grabbed his thirty-five-millimetre camera and shouted, "Lights, camera . . . *action!*" Making for the doorway, he said, "Come on, Caldwell."

"No, I'm . . ." Caldwell didn't know what he was.

"I need to get pretty pictures for the magazines," said Jimmy. "I need you to hold me."

There was another thunderclap. It rattled the molecules, shifting empty spaces from one end of the bar to the other.

"You go ahead, Mr. Caldwell," said Beverly. "It's not time, yet."

Caldwell backed off his stool.

Jimmy Newton put his shoulder against the door that led outside. He pushed and was met with steady resistance, the storm insisting, *No, no, you don't want to come out here.* "Give me a hand, Caldwell."

"Get out of the way," said Caldwell. Jimmy Newton moved to one side. Caldwell did a little skipping step, took a stride and then executed a small shuffle so that both feet pushed off at the same time. His right shoulder met the wood—a small rumble of thunder accented the contact—and the door popped open. Caldwell landed outside.

He was instantly soaking wet, his hair plastered down across his forehead. He felt a desire to take off his clothes, to stand up and meet the shower as though he'd just come off the soccer field, or from the hockey rink.

Newton scurried out, hunched over and trying as best he could to cover his camera with his upper body. "Hooeyy!" he screamed, exhilarated. "A fulguration!"

Lightning cracked the air, and although the thunder that accompanied it was rowdy and bullying, the electricity itself seemed as fragile as the world it shattered. It buzzed, thin sprays, and went away. An inverted tree of turquoise luminescence vanished a moment after it appeared, and then there was another. They reminded Caldwell of the beautiful pale blue webbing Jaime's veins made in her breasts while she was pregnant with Andy.

Caldwell wanted the lightning to hit him, to embrace him with crackling energy. He knew it wouldn't, because he had been around the world daring it to do so, and it had come nowhere near (except, of course, for that first bolt). For one thing—this was science—usually lightning doesn't meet the earth, despite all appearances. Most of it rips through the sky, connecting with other shoots, and although ultimately one of these might touch something, a tree perhaps, it is like the ball carrier, and the rest of the team merely cheers and vanishes.

Neither was lightning a constant, or even usual, companion to a hurricane. When there was, in Newton's argot, a "light show," Caldwell would grow quite optimistic, despite his lack of faith. He'd race outside to undertake some self-assigned duty, which the other chasers, the weather weenies, mistook for bravery. "There's a woman in that car over there!" "There might be someone in that house!" But most times he emerged from the hotel, the light show stopped almost immediately.

Caldwell had to confess that he was not single-minded in his pursuit of lightning. True, he sometimes travelled to places like Washington State, had once even paid a forest ranger thousands of dollars so that he might take his place for a week and sit up in the high tower. But Caldwell also knew that southern Ontario experiences as much lightning as anywhere on the globe, if not more; if Caldwell were really serious about the stuff, he'd stay put. Near home. He was unwilling to do this, of course. So he hunted hurricanes.

Caldwell had never been drawn to tornadoes, though he had been interested in the newspaper reports of destruction, even devastation. Sometimes they came in gangs, thirty or forty of them lighting upon the earth. One such attack in Pennsylvania, in 1985, did damage totalling $450 million. It put a thousand people in hospital and killed seventy-five. Caldwell's own hometown of Barrie had been set upon by a rogue tornado. The twister swept across Highway 400, picking up cars and tossing them aside. It came at Barrie Raceway and took the horses up into the clouds. Several people died, although at the time Caldwell hadn't paid much attention; his own family was spared, after all. Jaime and Andy were at home, miles away from the tornado's path. After the hole in Caldwell's life, he had heard about the Weather Watcher Tours through Tornado Alley, but it wasn't what he wanted. He had an image of himself in a farmer's field, dodging and darting like a defenceman on the blue line, watching the twister's every move warily, trying to get in its way. Hurricanes were bigger; once tracked down, Caldwell had only to stand still.

"Okay, baby!" shouted Jimmy Newton. He ran down the little rise, where Lester had splinted the striplings. The wind had driven the plants parallel to the ground; Lester's splints had cracked near the bottom but were still fast to the little trees with twist-ties.

Jimmy stopped halfway and the wind pushed him over sideways. He landed on his ass and elbows, his hands still tight around the camera. "Pick me up, pick me up, pick me up," he giggled. Caldwell put his hands in Jimmy's armpits and drew him skyward. There was a lightning bolt then, close enough that Newton started, but Caldwell wasn't impressed. He wrapped his arms around Newton's shoulders and then set himself, one leg back, the foot twisted sideways for purchase, the other leg locked forward.

"Okee-dokee." Jimmy took his camera into his hands, raised it up, wiped rain from the tiny viewer and peered through. He aimed it at a naked palm tree that shook ecstatically. At the shore, Maywell's boat twisted on its moorings, colliding with the wooden pylons like a wild horse bucking inside a stall. Jimmy depressed the shutter, muttered, "*Another* fucking Pulitzer Prize."

And this was the *leeward* side, Caldwell noted calmly. The storm was actually broadsiding the other side of Dampier Cay. Jimmy Newton seemed to have the same thought, because he batted Caldwell's arms away, turned and began to make his way across the flagstone patio. Caldwell followed. The two men lowered their heads, bent forward and planted their feet with plodding intensity. Even though the patio was only twenty-odd feet across, these yards were hard won, and when Caldwell reached the other side, he was tempted to raise his arms above his head in triumph.

Caldwell had not wanted to be a professional athlete, not even in his teens, when he might reasonably have dreamt such dreams. He played junior hockey, after all, for the Barrie Blades. This was how his family had ended up in Barrie; the Caldwells, as a clan, had nothing going for them except their fifteen-year-old son's burgeoning hockey career.

Caldwell took hold of Jimmy's shoulders, braced himself against the wind. Newton raised the camera, aimed it at the sea. The long metal lens protector was useless here, rain finding its way down the shaft and onto the glass. Jimmy didn't seem to care; after clicking the shutter a few times, he lowered the camera and simply stared at the approaching storm.

Newton half turned his head and called back, "Hey, Caldwell. Suppose the surge clears this cliff?"

Caldwell peered over the side. "You think it might?"

"Wouldn't that be fricking *awesome?*"

Though Caldwell had never wanted to be a professional athlete, on some level he had always wanted to be a phys. ed. teacher. Even as a teenager he had dressed like one, wearing grey slacks and white golf shirts while his friends wore jeans and T-shirts. Where their hair was long and messy, he kept his neatly trimmed, his instinct being to keep himself as plain as possible.

Jaime had wanted to be a phys. ed. teacher too.

They met at the University of Western Ontario, both attending, on the first day of their university careers, a class in kinesthiology. It bewildered Caldwell to be attending a class in kinesthiology, because in the back of his mind he was already a phys. ed. teacher, and needed only to have the silver whistle hung about his neck. But now he found himself in a class-room, the rows of study tables raked precipitously. All around there were illustrations of naked human bodies, many more than naked, reduced to bands of muscle and connective tissue. The professor was a disappointingly small man, disappointing because Caldwell had assumed that all of the teaching would be done by phys. ed. teachers, über–phys. ed. teachers, remark-able specimens in blindingly white golf shirts.

Caldwell was drifting off—he'd had too much beer the night before, chumming about with others in the physical education program, young men who, like him, seemed always destined to become phys. ed. teachers—when the door behind the professor opened and this girl walked through. The other students had entered from doors up above, filtering down through the aisles. This girl had obviously been battling through unknown subterranean territory; she barged through the door and was therefore the subject of the professor's pointer when he said the words "a strong, healthy human body."

The students laughed, the humour here being that the phrase was so obviously applicable. The girl radiated good health, as though she'd been some test subject, reared in a laboratory in the bowels of the building, milk-fed and exercised, and was just now being set free in the world. She said, "Gee, thanks," which redoubled the students' laughter, and the professor, perhaps angered by this, said, "You're late."

"I got lost," she said. Caldwell would reflect later that this statement wasn't precisely true. Jaime was always claiming to be lost, to have gotten lost, but what she really meant was that she'd made no great effort to discover where she was or where she was going, preferring to set out into the world with the naive innocence of a seventeenth-century explorer. So, in reading her schedule that day, Jaime had only noted the building and room number.

"Don't be late again," the professor cautioned, and the girl nodded, as though striking a bargain, and then mounted the risers two at a time, entering the same row as Caldwell and sitting down immediately beside him.

"What have we learned so far?" she whispered. She was busily arranging stuff on the workspace, which pulled up and folded out. She put her notebook there, a pen, a pencil, an eraser. Caldwell had set out none of these things and realized, when she asked the question, that he had no idea what he'd learned thus far. Probably nothing. He desperately tried to remember, because he'd been paying attention, at least he was pretty certain he had. There was something about ligaments or ligatures or something. He knew this wasn't good enough to present to the girl, who had pushed her short brown hair back behind her ears in order to listen better. He considered a response like "Sweet dick-all," which he would have uttered without hesitation if it had been a guy sitting down beside him. By this time, of course, the girl thought he was an idiot anyway, because he hadn't spoken. So he said what he figured would make the best locker-room story. And although Jaime made much hay of the fact that the first words he ever spoke to her were, "Would you like to go out with me?" she never suspected that they represented more truly her first encounter with Caldwell the A-hole.

THE DOOR BLASTED OPEN and Caldwell and Jimmy Newton blew back into the Pirate's Lair. They were soaking wet, their hair and clothes disarranged and tumbled. "Holy Christ," Jimmy said, waving his little arms in the air, "she's the biggest thing I've ever seen and she's not even fucking *here*."

Gail scowled, shook her head. "Of course it's *here*. Just listen to it."

Beverly did just that, closing her eyes and tilting her head to listen to the song of lost souls.

"Hey," demanded Gail, and Beverly popped open her eyes. Gail stood in front of her, her arms crossed sternly across her chest. "What are you smiling about?"

"I'm sorry," said Beverly, "I was just thinking."

"You people . . ." Gail pointed to Jimmy, Caldwell and Beverly. "You people kind of creep me out."

"How so?" asked Beverly.

Sorvig answered, "Because you want to get *dead*."

Newton rubbed his head with a bar towel and patted his thin hair back into position. "Not me," he said. "There's some danger involved, sometimes, but it's like any, you know, *extreme* activity. Haven't you ever done anything risky?"

"Not really," said Gail.

"Okay, here's the thing," said Jimmy. "You know what a tsunami is?"

"Sure," said Sorvig.

Gail nodded. "Tidal wave."

"Now *that* is power. A tsunami is the whole ocean coming at you." Jimmy held his hands one above the other to illustrate compression, bringing them together, pulling them apart. "You know, if a tsunami starts like a hundred miles offshore, there's only maybe seven actual wave actions before it hits land. Think about that. You know what happens before a tidal wave comes? The water disappears. Harbours just suddenly go bone dry. Then the wave arrives. A wall of water a hundred feet tall." Newton shook his head wistfully. "And sometimes I think about that moment, you know, the moment just before the tsunami hits. I think how wonderful it would be to be standing there in that moment, looking up at it. But I know the next moment wouldn't be so wonderful. So I try to see how close I can get to the one moment without getting my ass kicked the next."

"Myself," said Beverly, "I'm interested in what happens *between* those two moments."

"Well, like I mentioned," said Jimmy, "you're just a little bit nuts."

"Mm-hmm," agreed Beverly. "That would seem to be the general consensus."

"What is it exactly," Dr. Noth had demanded, repositioning her notepad upon her wide lap, gripping the arms of her chair to haul her bulk forward—they were obviously getting down to the heart of the matter—"that you think you want of these encounters?" Dr. Noth was referring to the more furtive acts that Beverly had spoken of: prowling the streets of Orillia on stormy nights, poking her head inside bus shelters to see who was standing in the shadows.

Dr. Noth irritated her more than most of the professionals. She had an odd odour and an unrelenting hunger for what she considered "answers." Beverly pursed her mouth for a moment before answering. "I don't suppose I want anything other than the encounter."

"But what do you think is the significance of the weather?"

"Hmmm, interesting." Beverly often said that when sitting with Dr. Noth; the woman never noted the sarcasm. Beverly touched a finger to her face, as though giving the question serious thought. "Well, you know, there may be a biophysical significance. It may well have to do with ionization. People find storms exciting. Energizing."

"And when energized, you feel the need to make these sexual connections with total strangers?"

"Well, I don't have a very wide circle of acquaintances."

Dr. Noth wrote something down then, what exactly Beverly couldn't guess. Beverly knew that she was a prize case for Dr. Noth, a history that the doctor intended to write up for some medical journal. There were so many tragedies in Beverly's life that determining the root cause of her behaviour was, to a psychologist, what proving Fermat's theorem was to a mathematician. Some professionals fastened onto the murder-suicide of her parents. Others asked endless questions about her grandfather, searching for signs of sexual abuse. And of course there were many who pointed their fingers at the death of Margaret, beautiful little Margaret of the long golden hair.

The way Beverly behaved bewildered her as much as it did anyone. She functioned well enough at work. Even Mr. Tovell, who did not like Beverly on some profound level, was willing to admit that she was efficient. Their office was a small branch of a large multinational concern, and Beverly's main job was filing. She actually had the same problem with this as she had with grocery bag stuffing; there was usually something left over, a sheaf of papers in her hand for which there was no room in the cabinet. Beverly would then place it somewhere arbitrarily—or not quite arbitrarily, there was some sort of logic operating—and she maintained her reputation for efficiency by remembering where these things were. "Bring me the Donlands file," Mr. Tovell would bark, when other staff had failed to locate the thing in the *D*s. Beverly would hurry away and dig through the *M*s, because when she was a little girl, milk had been delivered by Donlands Dairy.

This was how she usually got through the workday. After Margaret died, she moved to a flat above a store that sold uniforms, things like nurses' outfits and white shoes with thick soles. She would mount the stairs to her apartment, which consisted of two rooms, a bedroom and a kitchen. The bedroom contained a bed, a standing closet, a small chest of drawers. In the kitchen was an old fridge that usually held some fruit and cartons of milk in various stages of souring. There was a tiny television set on the counter, and on the kitchen table was Beverly's computer. As soon as she entered her apartment, she pressed the "on" button, and as the machine booted up, she threw off her work clothes. She would put on a T-shirt and sit down behind the keyboard.

Then she would click the icon that connected her with the Internet. Nightly she visited various sites pertaining to weather and storm tracking. She would stare at satellite photographs, squinting to simplify the masses of white, looking for big formations.

One day she saw a puff of white obscuring the Cape Verde islands, off the west coast of Africa. This excited her, even though she knew it was commonplace. But it was the beginning of September, the start of hurricane season, and perhaps her excitement was akin to the optimism a fisherman feels on opening day, an optimism that no amount of past failure can diminish. The next day this little button of white had grown larger, moved slightly toward the Americas. She checked with NOAA's site, noted that it had achieved official depression status. She touched the little patch of white and pulled her finger across the computer's screen, not thinking, only reacting to ethereal whim, and when her finger passed over a tiny sliver of black, she had enlarged the image. Another option laid a gridwork overtop the image, words appearing beside the various formations. *Dampier Cay*.

Now, as the hurricane neared, as Caldwell once again took a seat on the bar stool beside her, an answer occurred to Beverly. She felt an urge to telephone Dr. Noth, but there were no telephones at the Water's Edge. And whatever phones *were* on Dampier Cay were going to become useless very soon. But if she could have spoken to the professional, Beverly would have said, "It's easy to see what I want. I'm looking for someone who is looking for the same thing."

———

After that class in kinesthiology, Caldwell went to the Olympic-size pool in the college's athletic centre. He found an empty lane and dove in, and for half an hour he went up and down the right-hand side. He was not a particularly good swimmer, but he could go for very long distances. In the back of his mind he had always imagined attempting some marathon journey, across Lake Simcoe or something. He had done this since he was a child, although as a child he had dreamt of stepping into familiar water and swimming to some other shore where everything was new and unknown.

As he neared the wall in the deep end, he heard a voice say, "Excuse me." Caldwell did not suspect that it was directed at him, since he was minding his own business. So he turned and did another two lengths, up and back. This time the voice was brittle. "*Excuse* me." Caldwell stopped mid-turn, pushing off the wall and then waving his arms to slow his progress. He turned and saw a woman standing above him.

This image Caldwell kept with him. In the days before the hole in his life, it was always close at hand. Caldwell used it sometimes as he and Jaime were making love, especially as the end neared, when Jaime had come and Caldwell was free to charge at the finishing line like the huge clumsy athlete he was. After his memory was destroyed, the image would occur randomly, unbidden, and he would have to stop whatever he was doing.

As Caldwell looked up at her, Jaime's thighs appeared even more massive than they really were. She was a competitive swimmer, and her hours in the pool had exaggerated her body in many ways. Her thighs wowed, ballooned with muscle. She wore a black bathing suit, modestly cut, the bottom drawing a prudish line across the top of her legs, the top wrapping around her neck almost clerically. But she had raced through the showers on her way poolside, and the wet material clung to her little belly and her breasts.

So Caldwell pulled off his goggles and this image burned itself into his memory.

"The thing is," Jaime said, and she lifted her hand and began to make a circular motion, "you're supposed to do laps in the lane. You know. Up the right-hand side, down the left-hand side. That way, three, even four people could use the same one."

"Seriously," said Caldwell, "I think we ought to go out together."

Jaime had been gazing at the pool and organizing it theoretically, but now she looked down and saw who it was. It took a moment, but a smile did come. "Oh, why not?" she muttered. Then she dove in. Caldwell watched as she moved underwater, like a dolphin, her body undulating and rippling with strength. She broke the surface about halfway down the pool's length and began a fierce crawl.

Caldwell leapt off his bar stool suddenly. He looked at Beverly and smiled. "I have to go do something," he said. He bent over and kissed Beverly on the lips, as lightly as he could manage, and then he left the Pirate's Lair.

Jimmy Newton picked up the digital video camera, aimed it at the people in the Pirate's Lair. There was a light on top, a lamp that sent out a strong beam, and people would squint and scowl as the thing was aimed at them. Especially Maywell, who usually squinted and scowled. "Get that thing away from me."

"We're going out live all across the world," said Jimmy. "Anybody you want to say hello to?"

"No." The only person who meant anything to Maywell was in the same room.

Jimmy moved on. "Sorvig?"

Sorvig, after thinking for a moment, waved at the camera and then began to speak a strange language. Beverly listened for words she might recognize. In a certain mood she felt she could understand people no matter what language they spoke, because words were really not as powerful as everyone imagined. They were weak, rusty and old-fashioned locks that could be popped open with hairpins.

In fact, Sorvig did use some words that Beverly recognized, English words. "Sunbathing," she said, and "hurricane." Beverly wondered about the country Sorvig came from, which lacked expressions for these things, some vacuum of a place where there was no light or wind.

Jimmy aimed the camera at Sorvig's friend. "How about you, Gail?"

"Well, um, hi, I guess, *Cheryl*. Wish you were here." Gail and Sorvig both laughed for a short time and then fell silent.

"Crazy lady? I mean, Beverly?"

Was there anyone Beverly wanted, *needed*, to say hello to? Not her grandfather, certainly. Beverly didn't hate her grandfather, but she was certainly angry with him most of the time, resentful of his resentment. He resented her, of course, because she'd survived her mother, because when the police finally burst through the door, little Beverly was sitting in her high chair, apparently gurgling happily. Perhaps her grandfather resented that, the happy gurgling, but Beverly suspected the old man had made up that piece of the story, justification for his resentment.

If not her grandfather, then who? It suddenly struck Beverly as funny, *humorous,* that there was no one else in the world with whom she had any connection. She had not been distant, she had not been aloof—in fact, she'd been the furthest thing from aloof—and yet, there was no one.

Still, it seemed fitting to say something, to make some sort of announcement. "I'll send a big hello to anyone out there," said Beverly, "who has lost someone. Maybe that's most everybody, I don't know. It's a lot of people. And I just wanted to point out that maybe they're not really lost, I mean *gone.* Because when you think about it . . ." Beverly lifted a hand in the air, began to turn it around in a slow circle—cyclonic action. "Sometimes everything—people and time and *everything*—gets sucked up by a storm. A hurricane or a tornado. And it might seem like you've lost something, but you haven't, when you think about it, not if you get sucked up by the same storm, you see what I mean, maybe you can't get at it, but it's not *lost,* you're part of the same, it's there and you're here and everything goes round and round so that . . . Oh fuck, where is Mr. Caldwell?"

The mechanics of fly casting are simple; many people, even non-anglers, are familiar with the concept that the rod is stopped, forward and back, on the face of a huge imaginary clock—one o'clock, eleven o'clock. This is how Caldwell had learned, but he didn't conceive of casting that way any more, because it involved time. He preferred a conceptualization that had been suggested by a particularly grizzled guide in New Zealand: "You're standing in the middle of an empty room with a paintbrush. Now, flick paint on the wall in front of you. Now on the wall behind." This appealed to him for the sense of destructive mischievousness it lent to casting. But Caldwell's favourite little mantra, the one he employed now, was "Hurl the hatchet" for the forward cast, and for the back, "Stab the sky." Actually, he didn't even bother with "Hurl the hatchet" most of the time, and he would mutter, over and over again, "Stab the sky. Stab the sky. Stab the sky."

Of course, none of these are any use at all when hurricane-force winds are involved. That didn't stop Caldwell. Lightning still sparked. The bolts were more infrequent but also more substantial, and Caldwell had hopes of hooking into one. So he stood on the rocks overlooking the ocean, staring into the face of Claire. He had found a flat surface, lower than much of the rise, only twelve, thirteen feet above sea level. The ocean exploded all around him, and once or twice spilled over and formed tentacles, wrapping around his ankles, trying to pull him away. Caldwell held fast, and, strangely, it wasn't that difficult. The undertow, that phenomenon so feared by Beverly, had been tamed by the storm. Nature operates by balance and equiponderance. So when waves come ashore, the water molecules floundering on land must be replaced out in the deep; this is why the undertow comes into being. Hurricane Claire was driving *all* of the water toward Dampier

Cay. She was supplying any deficit, so Caldwell found it relatively easy to keep his footing, even on the slick rock.

The actual casting was considerably more difficult. Caldwell held the rod upright, as best he could. The tendons in his forearm were puffed, the veins engorged, it felt as though his right arm might explode. The flyline was frozen behind him, describing a perfectly straight line perpendicular to the earth, virtually motionless. But Claire was almost done with thunder and lightning, as far as Dampier Cay was concerned. She would now use her two main powers: wind and, the greater one, water.

"Mr. Caldwell?"

Caldwell turned, and in that tiny moment of distraction the wind took his rod away. It flew like an arrow, sixty, seventy feet to the main building, striking one of the plywood boards that covered the dining-room windows, exploding into splinters. The storm had arrived.

Beverly was standing a few feet behind him. Caldwell turned and spent a long moment looking into her eyes. He understood what she was searching for.

Beverly said, "It's time."

MR. WEATHER WAS READY to do his stuff.

Jimmy had a computer bag slung over his shoulder, his laptop nestled in there, humming with battery power. The camera was wired to both the digital videocam and a transmitter that sent out a radio signal, and Newton had high hopes that the strange little metal tower in the centre of the dining room would fling this signal around the globe. Weather weenies everywhere could experience Hurricane Claire first-hand. But deep down he didn't care if the technology betrayed him or not. He was here, that's all that really mattered.

Newton wobbled toward the door. He stopped and twisted his body, trying to shift all the gear, looking for balance and comfort. Everything was mighty cumbersome. The transmitter, the size of a paperback book, seemed to weigh about twenty pounds. What the fuck did they make it out of, kryptonite?

What he needed, Jimmy decided, was an equipment caddy, someone to tote the peripherals. If Caldwell had stuck around, Jimmy would have asked him, but Caldwell was being weird; he was off fishing in the hurricane. Jimmy had seen him do this before. He'd spotted Caldwell standing in front of a monster storm surge with a fishing pole, poking at the sky, trying to get it to spit electricity. The man was fucking nuts, but let's face it, no weather weenie is a poster boy for mental health.

Caldwell only *didn't* disappear, reflected Newton, when there was some sort of actual emergency to deal with. Caldwell liked to play hero. One time—Newton ran through the catalogue in his head and decided it was Hurricane Francine—everyone was gathered in a big hotel in . . . someplace. He wasn't so good at remembering place names. It was a Third World country, Newton knew that, because although the hotel was tall and grand, it sat in the middle of a *village,* the houses small and wooden and not very well put together. Most of the villagers had come over to the hotel, where management grudgingly let them gather in the expansive lobby. The people seemed very happy there. They gossiped and played cards, and several men formed a circle and played some game that involved stones, throwing them on the floor and then exchanging coins. The watchers had commandeered their own little area, near a large plate glass window that rattled in its housing. This made the manager nervous, and he kept trying to lure the weather tourists away with promises of fine food and free drinks, but the weenies stood their ground. It's not like Francine was much of a storm—she barely made "two" status.

Anyway, they were looking through the window—Newton was recording the destruction of the villagers' houses—when a woman appeared at the doorway of one of the little shacks. They couldn't hear her, but it was clear she was screaming, her mouth forming a rictus of tormented fear. And Caldwell bolted out of the hotel. They all watched him struggle across the road. When he reached the woman, she gesticulated frantically at the shadows behind her. Caldwell dashed into the place just as the winds destroyed it. The planks and shingles flew away, and when they were gone, Caldwell stood there with a small child cradled in his arms. There was a big gash on his forehead and his nose was broken. All the weather watchers cheered. Caldwell, carrying the child in one arm now, stepped out of the debris and put the other around the woman's shoulder. She leant into him and Caldwell brought them back to the hotel.

But there was no Caldwell now, and it was time for Mr. Weather to deliver the goods, live coverage of the actual hurricane. Jimmy had an idea then, and he jerked his head up. He was a little startled to find Maywell Hope already looking at him. Hope's eyes were hard, the wrinkles around them laced together tightly. "No," said Maywell.

"Hey," protested Newton, "I'm a guest of the Water's Edge. I'm your responsibility."

"That's right, you're my responsibility," agreed Maywell. "So keep your butt parked here."

"Hey," snapped Jimmy, "I am a, a, *videographer*. I need to record this storm. For posterity. For *science*. So they can study the storm."

Hope wished to God that he had something to smoke.

Jimmy Newton decided to hammer home the point that recording the tempest would ultimately benefit mankind. "You know," he said, "they think that a hurricane isn't *a* storm, you see what I mean, they think it's more like a lot of storms. A lot of twisters within the main system, but they're not sure how they're organized. So if the scientists, like my buddies at NOAA, had footage to study . . ." Newton spread his hands, as though to illustrate the obviousness of his thinking. "Come on," he said to Maywell. "Night's coming. There's not much light left anyway."

Maywell was thinking that there must be a pack of cigarettes somewhere. He'd quit smoking a few months back, at least he'd told Polly at the time that he'd stopped forever, and during those torturous four days he'd secreted decks of smokes everywhere. "Go ahead, then, sir," he snapped. "Go film your storm."

"The thing is, Maywell," said Jimmy Newton, "I need your help. If you could just carry some of this stuff for me . . ."

The word "help" preyed upon Maywell. After all, he'd been off-island when storms had come before. Now it was time for him to climb up into the mast-riggings with all the other pirates. "All right, Newton," he said. "We'll go do what you have to do. After that, we come back in here and ride the damn thing out. Do we have a deal?"

Jimmy Newton extended his hand, then drew it back when it became clear no shaking was to be done. "Deal," he said.

Caldwell took Beverly's hand and they set off for the cottages, "J" and "K." The wind was to their back; they managed only a few steps and then were bowled over. Beverly and Caldwell wrapped their arms around each other and brought their mouths together. They both tasted blood.

Caldwell climbed to his feet and Beverly used him for purchase, digging her fingers under the waistband of his shorts, pulling herself upwards. She took hold of his chest, scratching him with her nails. And then she was upright, leaning into Caldwell's body, which was large and muscled and seemed, for the moment, to be equal to the storm.

"Your place or mine?" she screamed, her voice barely piercing Claire's roar.

Caldwell looked at the little harbour. Maywell's boat had been thrown up onto the dock, and was lying on its side injured, dying. Caldwell noted that water had swamped the piers. He tried to determine if it was high tide. He, Beverly and Maywell had gone fishing with the incoming tide—the bonefish creeping up, with the rising water, onto the shrimp-filled flats—so Caldwell began to add fours (four hours to high tide, four hours back to low, etc.) and concluded that high tide had yet to arrive. The main storm surge, he knew, would come behind the eye of the hurricane, so the fact that Claire had already pushed so much of the ocean at them was startling.

Alarming, even. If high tide coincided with the storm surge . . . A tiny knot of fear appeared in Caldwell's belly, the first palpable emotion he'd felt in years.

Caldwell suddenly realized that he was once again living in time. He hadn't lived in time since that Saturday morning so long ago, which had been punctuated by looking at wall clocks, checking his watch, calculating Jaime's whereabouts, wondering when Darla Featherstone might arrive with her camera crew. After that, he had become a stranger in time. He would wander about the world, only bumping into time occasionally. A bartender might call time. A hotel clerk might point to a seat in the lounge, telling Caldwell that he would have to wait, that it was not check-in time. And, of course, Caldwell was always missing check-*out*, management gleefully adding another day's rent to the tally. The world Caldwell had lived in for the past few years was defined neither by time nor by geography; it was informed by the elements.

Beverly took his hand and they completed their journey, running toward their twinned cottages. Beverly stopped outside the sliding glass door of "K." The council trees around the place shivered with frenzy. She took hold of the handle and tried to pull the glass door open, but she couldn't budge it. So Caldwell put his hand over hers, and together they moved the thing a foot to the left. Beverly slipped in first, then Caldwell. He pulled the door shut, turned, and Beverly fell into his arms.

"Let's dance," she whispered, or at least the volume of her voice passed for a whisper. The cottage was not very well constructed, and the wind found its way through the far wall. If outside there was howling, inside "K" there was sighing.

"Okay," said Caldwell. Beverly and he linked left hands, placed the right on the small of the other's back. They began to move about the room. Caldwell was awkward and bumped into things. Beverly rested her head on his shoulder, touched her lips to his neck. Caldwell turned his head slightly; Beverly's hair smelled of sea spray.

"I think we should get out of these wet things." Beverly kissed his neck with some firmness now, signalling a break with the authority of a boxing ref separating two fighters from a clinch.

She stepped back from Caldwell and kicked off her shoes, white runners made dingy by sand and dirt. Then she undid her green shorts and stepped out of them. She pulled her underwear off and straightened up. Caldwell saw that her pubic hair was light and downy. He had always found this exciting, nudity confined to a woman's lower half, and sometimes he asked Jaime to keep her pyjama top on when they made love.

Beverly reached down, crossing arms, taking hold of the bottom of her T-shirt. She pulled up. Her breasts were small, certainly much smaller than Jaime's, but they had a wonderful shape, with nipples that were almost crimson.

Caldwell hooked toes into heels and tossed his loafers into a corner. He removed his shorts and underwear as one. Beverly moved forward as soon as they hit the ground, reaching out and laying her soft palm upon his cock, which stirred with her touch. She stepped back and stared at Caldwell. He pulled off his own T-shirt. Beverly touched her fingertips to his pectorals, tracing their shape. Her hands came to rest above his nipples, and she pinched them, slowly increasing the pressure and then suddenly causing a little bolt of pain. Caldwell jerked, smiled and put his hands to her breasts, which were cool and smooth. The skin was especially soft on the outsides, and he brushed there with the sides of his callused fingers. He gingerly put thumbs and forefingers around her nipples; they hardened instantly, and, when he pinched, turned an even darker red. Beverly made a low humming noise and then said, "You have to tell me what you're thinking about."

Caldwell understood that she was giving him guidelines now, rules.

"I had to teach science to the boys," Caldwell told her. "I never really understood it, and I don't remember it now. I only remember a few weird facts."

"Such as?" Beverly stroked the back of his neck. She nuzzled in and kissed his chest, stretching upwards to lick his nipple.

"Well . . . you know what a lodestone is?"

Beverly stuck out her tongue and licked back and forth across Caldwell's nipple, and in doing so managed to shake her head no.

"Thousands of years ago they found these rocks, these stones, that were different from other stones in the world. The Chinese people called them loving stones, because they liked to kiss." Caldwell remembered that the boys in his science class used to snicker at this little aside, the same boys who grew bashful in health whenever he pointed at the diagram of the reproductive organs. "Sailors discovered that if they put these stones on a piece of wood and floated them in water, these rocks would point at Polaris, the lodestar, the star they used most for navigation. A lodestone was what we now call a piece of magnetite. But not just any piece of magnetite. It had to have a certain, um, crystalline structure." This was the sort of fact that Mr. Caldwell always barged by, ignoring. Although he knew it referred to matters microscopic, he imagined the stones were as cut and faceted as crystals from a chandelier in a fancy ballroom. "And something else had to happen for a piece of magnetite to become a lodestone," Caldwell said. "It had to be hit by lightning."

Beverly dropped to her knees and used a hand to direct Caldwell's penis into her mouth. Caldwell opened his own mouth, although he had yet to formulate the sentence he wanted to make. He knew it had something to do with futility. Perhaps he was going to echo the hooker Hester's sensitive observation that there was some problem with the hydraulics. But before he could say anything, his cock began to harden. He listened to the wind, which came in pulses and made his ears pop.

Beverly placed her hands on Caldwell's hips and straightened up a bit, to accommodate the increasing inclination of his cock. Her tongue retreated and she touched her teeth against his skin. Then she began to move her head up and down, chewing in the most delicate way, enough to suggest pain without inflicting it upon him.

A thought came to Caldwell then, although it's not accurate to portray this as any kind of epiphany. The thought had been his steady companion for many years, sitting across from him in various bars, sleeping in the other bed in sterile hotel rooms. Caldwell had been ignoring it all this time, lowering his eyes when it got too close. He tried to put distance between himself and the thought whenever he could find a storm. And the bigger the storm, the greater the distance; someday he would find a big enough storm that he and the thought would be separated forever.

The thought was, as you may have guessed, nothing but the simple reflection that he had loved his wife Jaime very, very much. And Andy, who was made of their love.

Something happened then, there in cottage "K." There was a low rumble, almost subsonic, a sound that crept beneath the ululation made by the wind. And then blue light pierced the wallboards, finding its way through the crooked imperfections. Everything in the room acquired an azure tinge: Beverly's hair, her hand around his cock, the very air. And then the cottage shook, so hard that the few pieces of furniture shifted position. Caldwell's ears popped and he was suddenly winded, working his mouth and lungs with the rhythmic desperation of a landed fish. Beverly released his cock and gulped for air. She seemed to notice the blue light then, turning her head first one way and then the other. There were only wisps of the strange light remaining, aquamarine filaments that were filtering back outside, sucked up once more by the cyclonic action.

"We were hit by lightning," said Caldwell.

"You figure?" Beverly backed up and sat down upon the bed. She spread her legs apart and leaned backwards, smiling at Caldwell. "That's good, right?"

"Yeah," nodded Caldwell. "It means we've turned into kissing stones."

Maywell donned foul-weather gear, a green plastic suit that looked laughably inadequate. He replaced his baseball cap with a sou'wester, knotting it beneath his chin with a neat little bow. Jimmy Newton gave Maywell the transmitter and the laptop computer to carry, both of which were wired to Jimmy's videocam, which meant that the two men were connected and had to stay no more than eight feet apart.

On his way out, Maywell stopped in front of Polly, like a schoolboy presenting himself to his mother.

"I won't be long," he said.

"I'll miss you."

Maywell opened his mouth to speak again but could find no words. He nodded, winked, turned to Jimmy. "Come on, then, Newton."

Jimmy stopped by the table where Gail and Sorvig sat. "I'll see you guys later," he said. The girls nodded and smiled a bit warily, because this guy was a furry little freak. For one thing, he was all jazzed up about the hurricane. For another, he was the most eligible guy there (which goes to show how far wrong Gail and Sorvig had gone in booking *this* holiday) and he hadn't even tried to cop a feel. They weren't particularly vain, either one of them, but they were well worth an end-of-the-world tumble.

Each woman felt this damned vacation was the other's fault, but what was the point in saying anything? They had

gone to their travel agent, who was a fairly cute guy named
Helmet, a name that afforded Gail and Sorvig great mirth.
They shared a giddy joke wherein "Helmet" referred to his
dick, which they imagined to be circumcised in an overem-
phasized manner. Anyway, they had gone to his office at lunch
hour, and while they talked with Helmet, both women
thumbed through glossy pamphlets from resorts with titles like
Sun & Sensuality. These places seemed perfect, just the ticket.
They existed on islands that Gail and Sorvig had heard of. The
pamphlets were full of pictures of people on the beach, in the
pool, at organized dances. Helmet told them he'd been to
many of the places and said they were big fun. *Totally happening* was the phrase he used, by which he implied, or maybe
they inferred, unbridled sexual excess, with guys like himself,
Gail and Sorvig imagined, Germanic sorts possessed of great
fleshy hammerheads. Then *one of them* (each thought it was
the other) had reached over and plucked up a cheesy mimeographed thing from a resort named Water's Edge that existed
on some island no one had ever heard of, Dampier Cay.

The building they were in was screaming. The wind
pushed and pulled at the plywood that covered the windows.
Rain forced its way through; although there were no gaping
holes anywhere to be seen, the floor of the dining area was
archipelagoed with puddles. From their table, Gail and
Sorvig could see down the passageway. Polly was in the dining room, mop in hand, although as soon as she dealt with a
puddle and turned away, it would reappear. Polly herself was
soaking wet, a real mess, but she laboured with concentration and industry.

"Come on, sit down, have a drink or something," Gail called to her.

"Yeah," said Sorvig, "it's not like what you're doing is making any difference."

"You've got to try to keep up!" Polly called back. "Otherwise things get out of hand."

Things were already pretty much out of hand. The building screamed, and even though at any one moment the screaming seemed as loud as it could possibly get, the next moment would bring an augmentation. Gail and Sorvig were both way past being frightened, they had left fear eating dust a long time back. They were numb inside now. Their emotions had coalesced into a shapeless glob that lay off to one side of their bellies like roadkill. Both wondered if the building could actually withstand the storm, but no way was either going to bring up that point. It was a *building,* after all, someone had actually *built* it. What would have been the point of building the thing if it couldn't stand up to what was, after all, just weather? Just fucking weather, that's all it was. Buildings were supposed to protect people from weather, and weather certainly wasn't supposed to pose a death threat. Gail and Sorvig lived in New York City, where night brought forth a horde of ghouls with ghastly intentions. They had survived that, and now their asses were grass because of *weather.*

Lester appeared in the Pirate's Lair. The girls didn't know where he'd been, not outside because he was still pretty dry. He brandished a hammer, his symbol of utility. Gail and Sorvig spoke as one, saying it before he could: "What will be, will be."

"Amen," said Lester. He went to the bar and stared at the wall there, the empty shelves, shelves that should have held liquor bottles shoulder to shoulder.

"Polly put them away somewhere," offered Sorvig.

"You don't need glass flying around," pointed out Gail.

They thought that Lester was at least halfway cool. True, he was on the far side of fifty, but he was in good shape, actually kind of astounding shape. All the guys at Planet Dickhead were always working out—the office tower had a fitness centre up on the thirty-fifth floor—but none of them had anything like Lester's muscle definition. And he could dance, a talent highly prized by Gail and Sorvig. The guys they knew, the guys the gaga gods had decided made up their so-called "dating pool," were all spastic.

"Besides," offered Gail, "you already got a pretty good buzz-on."

"Although," said Sorvig, "I wouldn't mind a little drink myself."

Gail nodded. "Me neither."

Lester swung around suddenly, as though trying to catch the liquor bottles in the act of tiptoeing toward the door. But Gail and Sorvig realized that he'd been distracted by a strange sound, an almost musical one, a raspy atonal yodelling.

"What's that?" asked the girls.

Lester thought about that, chewing on his lips. "The wind," he decided.

"Yeah, but," said Gail, "the wind and what?"

Lester squinted suspiciously. He raised the hammer and waved it in the air, slightly but threateningly, and went off as though in search of an intruder. Gail and Sorvig laughed, and that felt good, but they only laughed for a brief moment, because a realization was descending hard upon them both. Gail said it first: "I don't know if this building's going to make it."

Sorvig nodded, shook her head in dismay, nodded again. "Where should we go?"

Would the cottages be any safer? The main building was the most exposed to the onslaught, on the crest of the small rise. Their cottage was down the hillside a little, and maybe the wind wouldn't be so strong there.

Polly appeared beside the table, mop in hand. "Where's Lester?"

"Listen," said Sorvig, "we think maybe we should go somewhere else."

Polly frowned. "Why's that?"

"Because this place," said Gail, shrugging her shoulders to indicate the whole of the structure, "sounds like it's about to blow."

"Nonsense," said Polly. "Where's Lester?"

"He's gone off to fix something," answered Sorvig.

"What he should fix," Polly said, "is the covering to that big window in there. It's coming away on one side."

Gail and Sorvig nodded.

"Maywell hasn't come back yet." Polly made this both a statement and a question; there was an optimistic up-turn of inflection at the end of the statement, slight, just enough to elicit the response, "Yeah, he's come back, you just can't see him right now because he's . . ." wherever that might be. But Gail and Sorvig only glanced down at the tabletop.

"We're going to be fine," said Polly. "You two just relax."

"Okay," said Gail. "Okay," said Sorvig, although when Polly returned to her mopping, both girls rolled their eyes. "Yeah, right."

The door banged open and Jimmy Newton flew in backwards, covering a good ten feet in the air before landing. Gail and Sorvig were alarmed—Newton was allowing the fucking storm into the bar—but Maywell came through the door immediately afterwards, his hands still raised, his face still wrinkled by rage, and the girls understood that Newton's flight, although wind-assisted, had been effected by the Last of the Merry Boys.

"But you have to admit," said Jimmy Newton from the ground, "it was a fucking awesome shot."

"I admit no such thing," Maywell retorted, undoing the knot to his sou'wester. He pulled it from his head and shook water away. The hair underneath was matted, all of Hope's tufts and cowlicks tamed and lying flat. There was a gash on his forehead; blood mixed with water had made half of his face pinkish, and little rivulets of crimson webbed his cheek.

"Aw, what do *you* know?" said Newton testily, climbing to his feet. Sea water fell from them in steady streams.

They had begun, Hope and Jimmy, by circling the perimeter of the main building, clinging to the boarded walls. Newton filmed the palm trees, which were driven low to the ground, their branches waving like arms in supplication. Palms worship big storms, they have evolved so that when winds come, they quiver and kowtow.

The forest to the south of the Water's Edge was not doing as well. The trees there, oak and Burmese rosewood, were stronger, sturdier, and the storm was having her way with them. The trees were naked of foliage, delimbed, and some had already fallen. The dead trees had been blown up against others, and were helping push them over. "I need to get closer," Newton said to Maywell.

Maywell was squinting to the south. He'd fixed a hand under the brim of his seafarer's hat, to keep rain out of his eyes. He was trying to see Williamsville, which lay beyond the forest, but the air was too dark, the rain too heavy. "We'd have to go out in the open there," he said.

"That's kind of the point. Being out in the open."

Maywell thought about that, grunted.

"So let's go," said Jimmy, and together they left the meagre protection of the building. Maywell stood behind Jimmy, his hands upon his shoulders. They were slapped and pitched into by the storm.

Jimmy raised the videocam and spoke as he filmed. "The winds are somewhere between eighty and ninety, I guess, gusting to a little over a ton. But the wall is still a long way off, so, man, there's some power on the way."

After that, they'd made it to the other side of the building, the one facing east, the one that was broadside to the storm. They stood backed against the wall there and stared at the scene before them. "Jesus H. Christ," marvelled Jimmy Newton, "would you look at that?"

The sea was higher than Maywell had ever seen her. Looking up and down the coastline, he saw that the water had already risen halfway up the cliffside, and the tide was still going *out*. Unlike Caldwell, Maywell had to do no calculating, his rhythms and the ocean's were tightly connected, his marrow knew the cycle.

"Oh, boy! I need this!" shouted Jimmy Newton, pushed up against the building by the wind. He took Maywell's hand as though they were schoolgirls in a playground and ran toward the water. As they neared the edge of the cliff, a huge gust rose and toppled them. Newton landed flat on his back, and crossed his arms over his chest, trying to protect the camera yoked about his neck.

Maywell struggled to his hands and knees, slapped at Jimmy's shoulder. "Come on," he snarled, not thinking about what they were doing, or why, only continuing on doggedly now that a course of action had been decided. He scuttled ahead commando-style. Reaching the cliff edge, he hooked his fingers over it, and only then did he cast a glance backwards to see if Newton was following.

As soon as Newton neared, Maywell reached out and dug his fingers into his collar, dragging him forward. The water was suddenly whipped into their faces, exploding off the rock face below. "You need that?" demanded Maywell. "Get it, then."

Newton drew the camera forward, wiped some rain away. He rested the machine on the ground in front of him and pressed a button. But Newton only let it run a moment or two, then he punched another that extinguished the little red "record" light.

"What's wrong?"

"I want to film the water actually coming at me," he shouted. Newton chinned himself forward, peered down the rock face. "I could get in there," he said. Some five feet below was a small crevice, a vee that nature had carved away. "I'll wedge myself in there, you keep a hold of me from up here, this is going to be a-fucking-mazing."

"It's dangerous," said Maywell, nodding toward the ocean. "She's riled."

"Arr, matey," growled Newton, giddy with excitement. He reversed himself, dangling his legs over the side of the cliff. His face was now only an inch or two away from Maywell's. Maywell reached out and put a hand on Newton's shoulder. He took hold of the material hard, and Newton slipped away. His head bobbed out of sight; Maywell was dragged forward, the rocks scraping at his belly, but he did not let go of the man.

Newton wedged his little feet into the crotch made by the outcroppings, folded himself up and pushed knees and elbows against the rock. The water pressed furiously against his feet, sometimes at his knees, occasionally rising as high as his belly. Maywell Hope was pulled forward, the whole of one arm hanging off the edge, his fingers still wrapped around the material of Newton's shirt.

Jimmy fumbled with his camera and raised it up. He didn't bother with the viewfinder, he didn't bother aiming the thing in any real way, he simply raised it as best he could and pressed the record button. He filmed dark water and black sky. The ocean bubbled and seethed.

Caldwell, as usual, had got the science wrong. Really, the undertow was not so much tamed by the storm as shackled. The world existed in massive imbalance, there was simply too much water for the undertow to deal with in its regular and workmanlike manner. That work was left to a much fiercer relative, the rip current. The rip current prowled the edge of the coastline, moving vast amounts of water along narrow, invisible channels, occasionally darting into land when it spied any kind of opportunity. Which it did now, and Jimmy Newton happened to be there. Suddenly the videographer's ankles were gripped as though by a huge hand and he was pulled out of his sheltering vee and dragged away toward the end of the world.

Maywell was taken too. In an instant he found himself in the water, his forehead stinging. But he had not let go of Newton, because it was not in his nature to let go of things. If he'd been given any sort of advance warning, of course, Maywell might have elected to let the storm take Jimmy Newton. But as it was, he ended up in the water too, being consumed by a huge beast. In a calmer sea he might have been pulled to the bottom by the computer, the transmitter in his pocket, but this water churned so madly that the weight didn't make much difference.

Maywell lashed out with his free hand, scraping the knuckles against a rock, slapping it wildly, making contact with another, somehow managing to take hold of something. In an instant he was stretched out, both shoulders almost popping out of their sockets. One hand held a rock, one hand held Jimmy Newton, and there was a long moment of pain so intense that he didn't even bother to scream. If he had screamed, his mouth would have filled up with water, and Maywell was very fearful of drowning, always had been. So he accepted this moment in silence, and then it was gone, and his body was folded back in on itself as though he were the bellows of a concertina, pulling Jimmy Newton into him, and then the two men were spat back at the rock face. They slammed against it, Maywell taking most of the punishment, his body acting as a cushion for Newton's. The two men were shoved back into the vee and Maywell ped- alled madly for purchase, and drove himself upwards. He managed to pull Newton up and threw him forward, and the two men ended up on top, clinging to the edge. There was a brief moment of relative safety then, during which Newton started giggling. He raised the videocam into the air. "Got it," said Jimmy.

"How bad is it?" asked Sorvig.

"Bad," said Maywell Hope.

"It's the greatest storm I've ever seen," Jimmy said. "It's small and tight, like Andrew. And it's coming fast."

"Coming?" repeated Gail. "That motherfucker's *here.*"

"The big winds," said Newton, "are going to be concen- trated around the eye-wall."

"The eye-wall," repeated Sorvig.

"The inside of this baby. The wall around the eye."

Polly joined them with her mop. She knew full well the futility of her labour, but she needed to keep the implement in her hands, a symbol of vigilance. "May," she said, "I want you to add some nails to those boards. I swear to God some of them have been sucked out."

Maywell looked around the place. "Polly, did you ever hap- pen to find any packets of smokes anywhere, almost as though someone had *hidden* them or something . . ."

"These ladies," said Polly, dropping a shoulder toward Gail and Sorvig, "are a little concerned. Perhaps you could attend to it now."

The lights went out.

The girls gave out a little yelp as darkness took over, even though there was not much of a grade between the new black and the gloom that had existed a few moments previously. Maywell was actually surprised that the electricity had lasted as long as it had. He suspected that the poles were down now, that the storm had worked one free of its posting and then they all came away.

The sound came once more, that of a dying animal or, more precisely, of a beast that refused to die even though its limbs were torn off and blood gushed from gaping wounds.

Sorvig could see down the connecting passageway and into the dining room. Light was pulsing in there, with the muscled insistence of a heart. She drew the others' attention to it.

Maywell Hope wondered if it could be the Corpus Sant. He'd read about the Corpus Sant in Dampier's book. "'A Corpus Sant is a certain small glittering Light,'" he quoted from memory. "'The height of the Storm is commonly over when the Corpus Sant is seen aloft.'" Maywell had always wanted to see the Corpus Sant, a creature rendered out of pure light.

"What *that* is," said Jimmy Newton, "is the boards about to tear away from the windows."

Maywell took a few steps down the passageway, the rest following quietly behind. He glanced into the dining room and saw that Newton, damn him, was correct—the storm was pulling away the edges of the protective plywood, allowing the light, the doomed twilight, to flicker into the dining room.

A new sound came, heard only faintly beneath the yowling of the wood, an arrhythmic banging.

"What's that?" whispered Gail. She had wrapped one of her hands around Sorvig's, her other hand clutching a clammy doughiness. She suspected it was Jimmy Newton, but it didn't really matter at this point.

"It's Lester," said Maywell. "Out there trying to fix things."

Even though Lester had his mouth full of nails, he was reciting the one-hundred-and-fifty-second psalm, the one he'd created sometime after his boy died. The psalm had come to him while he was sitting where the Royal Tavern used to be. He'd squatted among the debris and sucked at a bottle of rum, and the words filled his body and he spoke them aloud. *Oh, Lord, sometimes it seems as though You are very far away from us. You withhold from us Your bitter bosom. You give us not the holy teat.* Lester knew that the words were heaven-sent, because many of them baffled him. He had not been previously aware, for example, that the Almighty was possessed of teats, but it seemed to make sense.

Lester was being shoved up against the plywood, a sheet that was six feet long, four feet wide. There were many nails driven into it, but the wind was plucking up the edges and the nails were popping out. They popped out and disappeared, swallowed by the tempest. The nails Lester had in his mouth were longer, four inches, and the two he'd managed to drive in were indeed holding. He drew out another, but it was stolen by the storm. He was down to four. Maybe, he thought, if he could affix one to each corner of the plywood, things would be all right.

Lester jammed the nail into the corner of the plywood, twisting the point. Unfortunately, the nail was in his left hand, the hammer in his right, and the storm was pressing his chest up against the board. There was no way he could pound it. It occurred to him that if he turned around and put his back to the wall—and if he could manage to take the nail in his right hand, put the hammer in his left—he could perhaps swing across his body and get at the head.

He dragged the hand holding the hammer across his belly, the sharp corner of the nail remover scraping skin, drawing blood. That hand managed to get close to the one gripping the nail. Lester barked out some of the psalm, took a deep breath, closed his eyes, and managed to exchange the contents of each hand, and the moment after he did that, he flipped around so that he was backed up against the plywood and Hurricane Claire was slapping him across the face.

"Come on, motherfucker," muttered Lester. "Let's see the best you got." He was, at that moment, angry enough to deliver a few blows, swinging the hammer across his chest and banging at the plywood, at his hand, once or twice actually upon the nailhead. But the storm got its fingers underneath the wood, plucked out the nails, first at the bottom, then at the top. The wind slipped underneath and raced to the other end, and Lester could feel the loosening behind his back. The other end popped free and there were no longer any nails holding the protective sheet in place.

Lester dropped the hammer and spread his arms, pushing back as hard as he could. At some moments, moments so small that Lester could not conceive of them in terms of clock-governed time, the wind helped Lester stay in place. There were other moments when the wind tried to push him forward, moments when he was dragged upwards or driven down. Lester survived these, somehow, because Lester was angry and the storm could go fuck itself.

"But You have given us eyes," Lester shouted, "and we can behold Your bounty! In the smallest flower and in the tallest tree! In a drop of water and in the ocean swell! In the sweetest breeze and also in the Hurricane . . ."

And that's when Lester saw it, the stranger, something new in the dark hurly-burly. It appeared on the cliffside, some fifty feet away. The stranger, Lester sensed, had always been in the storm, waiting to be born, and when it met the rocks, it lashed out and grabbed hold. It materialized magically, spinning upwards and weaving seductively, like a snake responding to a flute played by a turbaned fakir. It was a black genie, Lester thought—although Jimmy Newton would identify the stranger as a *spawner* and even Caldwell could account for it in terms of book-learned science, a small tornado created by the hurricane.

That's what was coming at the building, and although it hardly came straight—it darted to and from, sometimes appeared even to back up—its intention was clear. The stranger was coming for Lester. "'Oh, Lord,'" he screamed, starting the one-hundred-and-fifty-second psalm from the top, "'sometimes it seems as though You are very far away from us . . .'"

🌴🌴🌴🌴🌴

"THE PEOPLE GATHERED ON THE BEACH, IN GALVESTON."
Beverly bit down on her lower lip. She made fists and
rammed them onto the mattress, raising herself up, lifting her
pelvis toward Caldwell. "There was a festive atmosphere.
Families came, as though to a great reunion, a celebration.
There were hot dog vendors and silhouette artists." Beverly,
gasping as Caldwell drove his tongue in deeper, fell backwards on the bed. She reached out, one hand finding the
coarse blanket and twisting. "Even though that morning . . .
what morning was it, Caldwell?"

Caldwell stopped for a moment. "September the eighth,"
he said. "Nineteen hundred."

"That is correct." The instant Caldwell reapplied his tongue,

Beverly shuddered. She raised her head so that she could look at his face. "I want you inside me," she said.

Caldwell stood up and walked to the foot of the bed. He spent a long moment looking at her. There was no light in the cottage, only a dull crepuscular glow. Caldwell was a darker shape in the darkness.

He put his hands on the little bed and crawled forward. He held himself over her; she threw her legs up and wrapped them around the small of his back. She pulled him down, and his cock slid gently into her.

"Even though the water already stood two feet deep in some sections of the city, the townspeople were not concerned," whispered Beverly. "They gathered at the beach and watched the water rise. Some children flew kites. Other children splashed about in the swells." Caldwell moved with a steady grace. She kept her feet locked across his back, and as he moved he lifted her effortlessly, as though she were weightless, no longer affected by gravity. "Hmmm," she moaned, "that's good."

Caldwell brought his mouth down upon Beverly's, and their tongues touched gently and then roughly, but Beverly shook her head, breaking the kiss. She touched his face and gently outlined the uneven shape of his nose, which had been broken repeatedly upon the fields of battle. "The man from the Weather Bureau drove his sulky up and down the beach, telling the people to go home, to seek shelter," she said. "He told the people who lived closest to the beach to get to higher ground."

She slipped an arm between herself and Caldwell, pushed at his chest and moved away from him. She raised herself up on her elbows, blew hair from her face. "Let me get on top," she said, and they changed positions on the tiny bed. Caldwell lay down and stared upwards. Beverly took hold of his dick and held it gently as she straddled him. She touched the end to the wet lips of her pussy and made tiny opposing circles with her hand and her hips. Caldwell groaned. He could see dark scratches on the ceiling overhead, and understood that the shingles had been torn away, that the wind was now working at the wood.

"Did you go down to the beach?" asked Beverly.

Caldwell was now a giant ache. He shook his head.

"Yes, you did," she told him. "You went down with your family."

Caldwell closed his eyes. "That's right," he said, and then he was released, then he was sucked up inside as though Beverly were a cyclone. "I went down to the beach with Jaime and Andy. To watch. Andy took his fishing pole, because he thought maybe the redfish might have been drawn in with the water. Jaime had her swimming costume with her. She was going to change in the bathhouses there . . ."

"Uh-uh, sorry," said Beverly. "They were all destroyed."

"That's right." Caldwell reached up and brushed his fingertips across Beverly's breasts, across her hard nipples. "Jaime didn't care. She just stripped off and changed into her suit right there."

"People must have thought she was *insane,*" Beverly said. She grabbed Caldwell's hand with both of hers, pressed herself against it. "I went down with Margaret," she told Caldwell. "I didn't think it was a good idea, but Margaret was adamant. You know, if that's what everybody was doing, well then, that's what Margaret had to do." Beverly began to lift and lower herself steadily. "She, too, wanted to splash about in the waves, but I told her, 'No. Your swimming isn't strong enough. You need more classes.'"

"Andy had some worms in his pocket," said Caldwell. A roof board flew away, then another, then another, the lumber leaving with exuberant shrieks, eager to join the flock of dead things that circled in the sky. "He threaded one on, cast as well as he could."

"Yes," said Beverly. She fell forward, her hands landing well beyond Caldwell's head, her left nipple falling softly upon his lips. He kissed it, his tongue tracing its shape. "Go on," said Beverly.

"I didn't think he'd catch anything, and I was worried that he'd be disappointed, but I saw the fishing line go tight, and damned if he didn't have a decent-size red on, maybe four pounds." Beverly twisted now so that her right breast swung across. Caldwell caught it with his mouth, sucked it in, bit down on the nipple.

"All right, all right," said Beverly. "Ummmm . . ." She spread out the fingers of one hand, seeking all the purchase she could. She guided the other between their bodies, her fingers coming to cup Caldwell's balls. "The man from the Weather Bureau advised everyone to go home." Beverly moved her hand so that her fingertips could reach her clitoris, she began to strum and thrum as though she were playing a musical instrument. "So I said, 'Margaret, let's go home . . .'" Beverly stopped speaking for a long moment, her fingers working frantically. Caldwell was pushing up with his hips, lifting her body toward the holes in the ceiling. The rain now poured through, the sheets were soaking wet, both Beverly and Caldwell glistened.

She was coming close to that place, she was nearing the edge of the cliff, but she did not want to go over, because something wasn't working. Actually, something was working all too well, better than Beverly could remember this sort of thing working.

"Jaime went for a swim." Caldwell pictured Jaime in her bathing costume. She splashed into the swells, her short hair standing on end and dancing madly. She lowered herself once, twice, three times; each time she rose from the surf, more and more of her bathing costume clung to her body. The first time she stood up, Caldwell could see the shape of her bush, then her rounded belly and finally her breasts. Jaime lifted her hands above her head and placed her palms against each other.

He reached forward and felt Beverly's ass, the muscles there. Her flesh was cooled by the wind and the rain inside the room. The wind was doing some damage. The mirror had been ripped from its place, the little table shattered against the wall.

"Jaime went for a swim, the crazy woman," said Caldwell. He imagined, maybe remembered, Jaime diving into the water. She began to swim toward the horizon. Jaime's specialty was the breaststroke, and one would have thought it useless against the unearthly tide, but Jaime swam away until Caldwell couldn't see her any more.

"And Andy was playing with all the other children." Caldwell didn't know where all the other children were, but he knew they were happy. "Margaret was playing with all the other children too," he said.

"Just be quiet and fuck me," said Beverly, though she herself was surprised to hear the words coming out of her mouth, "until I come."

THE CYCLONE picked up Lester and carried him away. He flipped and thrashed like a fish in a pelican's beak, and then he was spat out, thrown toward the rocks by the sea. This surprised him somewhat, to find himself so far away from the building. He was not frightened, simply surprised, even vaguely impressed. He prepared himself for a painful drop onto the boulders, drawing his elbows into his sides, balling his fists across his cheeks, protecting his eyes. But instead he landed in water, water that was warm and foamy. Lester was slammed up against the cliffside, although since there was only a drop of a few feet from rock to water, it could no longer be considered a cliffside. His fellow islanders could no longer consider the east side of Dampier Cay as any sort of protection because there was no longer a natural breakwall. This was information that Lester thought he should share with Maywell Hope. That notion, more than any sort of instinct for self-preservation, motivated Lester to attempt to extricate himself from the situation.

He reached up and tried to take hold of the rocks there, but they were rounded and slick, and his hands kept slipping away. They slipped away, and Lester would have to deal with the churning water, which treated him like a washing machine treats an old sock. He appraised the relationship of his frail body to the rock face by judging which part of him stung at any particular moment. Every time his face smarted, he calculated that it was time to act. Finally his left hand fumbled its way into a crevice. With his other hand he took hold of a small out-cropping, the point digging into his palm. Now it was time to pull himself up and over.

"Oh, Lord," Lester bellowed toward heaven, but suddenly he could no longer remember the words to the one-hundred-and-fifty-second psalm. "Oh, Lord," he began again, but it was no use. "Oh, Lord," he said, "are You going to help out or what?"

When the storm took Lester away and threw him into the angry ocean, the sheet of plywood he had been securing disappeared. It was gone in a trice, a vanishing as instant and magical as anything ever accomplished by a tuxedoed illusionist. That particular sheet of wood ended up in Burt Gilchrist's backyard, where it sawed off a tall birdhouse near the base, toppling it over. That birdhouse was fairly useless anyway. Burt and his wife had purchased it in Vermont, where they lived, and it was designed to serve songbirds. The huge waterfowl on Dampier Cay ignored it, for the most part, although once a cormorant had lighted on its roof, remaining there for a few hours, drying himself, standing first on one leg, its wings spread wide, then the other.

The Gilchrists' property was only a couple of miles away from the Water's Edge, but the storm was altogether different there—belligerent and bullying, but not deranged. Burt and his wife stood on their porch and watched the storm as night fell. Their clothes fluttered and the wind was too loud to speak above—which Burt considered something of a blessing—but they could hold on to the wooden pillars and see what the hurricane was up to. They watched as a sheet of plywood came flying through the air. It rippled a little, like a flying carpet. The board smacked their little birdhouse and the thing went down.

That was the worst that happened. The storm shutters were never really tested. Some water got into the laundry room, but the laundry room was designed to get wet now and then.

Still, their lives were ruined. Burt's wife—her name was Vera, née Dawson—was able to forgive Burt his dalliances with Doris Blembecker, but Burt couldn't get his head around the fact that Vera had slept with Pete Carney, his best fucking friend. Burt couldn't believe that Carney was capable of this act, and his anger with Vera had mostly to do with her having allowed the heartbreaking betrayal to take place.

Maywell Hope herded everyone down to one end of the Pirate's Lair, as far away from the bar, the windows, the passageway as they could get. The wind tore off more plywood sheets from the windows in the dining area, the panes of glass rattled and rippled.

It was deep night now, and they had given their hearts over to despair. Sorvig made deals with God, although she suspected He would never honour them. Gail went over a mental list of regrets, and what stung her most was how paltry these regrets were: breaking up with Josh over a misunderstanding, being too proud to take him back, that sort of thing. Gail had wasted her fucking life, which was bad enough, but this seemed such an awful way to die, destroyed by brutal bad luck.

Jimmy Newton lowered his head and listened to the storm, like a music lover might listen to a symphony, searching for nuances, variations on themes. He kept his thoughts to himself, but Maywell, studying Jimmy's face closely, seemed to read them. "What is it they say, Newton?" he demanded. "Mind what you wish for, you may get it."

"They say that," Jimmy agreed, trying to placate the pirate. But Newton had wished his whole life for this storm, and he had no problems with its arrival. He had no problems at all, no little human problems. He was not a pudgy little man who lacked social skills, he was Mr. Weather and he was in the middle of a beautiful storm, and that was all he'd ever wanted. So Jimmy listened as though the storm were a symphony, and in his heart he sang along.

Polly held Maywell's hand and remained calm, perfectly still. This was a monumental act of will, however, because it was not in her nature to remain still. She'd done what she could in terms of preparation—including ordering a radio tube from a supplier in Florida, paying for a plane ticket, dispatching Lester to fetch the thing—but now she could do no more. This desire to do, to fix, to be busy, bubbled away inside her, starting in her belly, rising to her chest, catching in her throat. And as it boiled away, this desire changed and became panic. Polly knew she would not be able to be still much longer.

The storm seemed to be following the builder's progress in reverse on cottages "J" and "K," removing the extra-structure first, tearing away the flimsy wallboards, making doors and windows disappear. Then it got to work on the wooden skeleton.

The joists were bound by tornado ties, and the storm had to work at these. Not for long, of course; Claire knew a little trick, which was to twist the four-by-fours in opposite directions until the metal connectors buckled and popped away.

"We went home late in the afternoon," said Caldwell, his words coming in short, airy bursts. "We lived on C Street." Galveston, Texas, was laid out in a very orderly manner, the avenues named alphabetically, proceeding from the beach. "You must have lived around there."

Beverly made no answer. Caldwell took hold of her thin waist and slowed the motion of his hips. "I used to see you sometimes, you and your daughter, walking along the streets. She had such beautiful hair. Long, golden hair."

The world around her was being destroyed by cyclonic action. Beverly had awaited this moment, spent money she didn't really have in order to find it. But now, when escape to Galveston was possible, she found herself tethered to the world by physical things: Caldwell's large hands, his muscled thighs, his thickly veined cock. Not that he was doing anything that hadn't been done before, or doing it with especial tenderness or ferocity. But he was doing it with uncommon need, a need that was almost infinite and served them both.

Maywell knew that something was up with Polly. He decided to distract her, although it was hard to arrive at a method. Polly and he didn't have a lot to say to each other, not that Maywell considered that a fault in their relationship. They both worked hard all day, made love quite a bit, and otherwise were silent and content in each other's company. So if Maywell were to pipe up now—ask a question about the running of the Edge, say—Polly would prickle up suspiciously and maybe lose what hold she had.

He considered telling Polly he loved her, which needed to be done sometime, and this seemed like the time, being as there might not be much left of it. He licked his lips, which were dry, made papery by the sun.

But before he could speak, Polly suddenly bolted down the passageway and into the dining area. Maywell was two steps behind her—two steps too many, he knew, he'd been caught napping, he'd been rendered insensible by his imperfect, pirate's love—and he put his hand on her shoulder, began to turn her around.

"Come on back, now," he said.

"I have to do *something* . . ."

The window exploded. Or imploded, really, sucked into the black hole of the dining area. The glass was pulverized, the molecules seeking release, freedom, escape. Tiny grains drove themselves into Maywell's face. There were some larger pieces in the air, though, oddly shaped triangles, and it was one of these that embedded itself in Polly's neck, severing the jugular vein. Her blood spouted into the air. She collapsed into Maywell's arms, and he dragged her back into the Pirate's Lair.

"We went home late in the afternoon," Caldwell continued. "Is that when you went home, Beverly? Anyway, Jaime, Andy and I went upstairs to the bedroom. The ground floor was covered by a foot of water. I thought, everyone in town thought, that that was as high as the water could rise."

Caldwell was standing now. Beverly had her arms wrapped around his shoulders, her legs around his waist. Sweat mixed with tears on her face.

"Bev? Do you remember what it was like? Sometime during the night the storm surge came. All at once the water appeared in our bedrooms, exploding up through the floorboards. Andy came running into our room, he climbed into bed with us. I didn't know what to do. The water kept rising. There was this banging sound, I wasn't sure what it was. I found out later it was the streetcar trestle, torn loose and battering the house. The house collapsed around us, and we—my family—floated away on the mattress. No one knows what became of us, our bodies were never found."

Maywell held his hand over Polly's wound, trying to clamp the vein together. Blood geysered through his fingers. "There's a first aid kit somewhere behind the bar," he said to Gail and Sorvig, and then he turned to Jimmy Newton. "Radio for help."

Jimmy reached into one of the pockets of his jacket, pulled out a flashlight, pressed a thin but strong beam of light into being.

"Why didn't you take that out before?" asked Sorvig.

"We didn't need it before," answered Newton.

"But don't you understand how much it would have meant to have light, just a little light?"

"Sorry," muttered Jimmy. "Now come on."

Newton and the girls headed toward the bar, pushing their way through the unruly storm that flooded down the passageway and into the Pirate's Lair.

As the girls found the little white tin box with the red cross on it, Newton aimed the flashlight at the radio. "Fuck," he sighed. He worked his way back, knelt down in the blood beside Maywell and Polly. "You want to get her head up, I think," said Jimmy. "Rest it on your lap there. Keep pressure on—"

"Did you make the radio call?"

"I can't. There's no electricity, there's no radio battery . . ."

"What the hell do you mean?"

"I mean—"

"Damn you, Newton."

"Look, Maywell, *I'm* not the guy who didn't put a battery in the frigging radio."

Maywell's face trembled and collapsed. "I don't understand such things," he confessed, and then his features went rigid once more.

"Okay, look, I brought a little portable generator up here."

"Get it."

"Yeah." Newton tried to remember, through the fear and the exhilaration, where the thing was. Somewhere in the dining room, he thought. A squat little machine with ports for two battery packs. Newton couldn't think why he'd left it in there, but he didn't suppose it mattered why. That's where the thing was. It was in the big room that Hurricane Claire was currently destroying.

He started for the dining room, crawling so as to be as small as possible, to present as little of himself to the fury. He knew that there was plenty wrong with the plan. For one thing, he didn't think anyone would be able to get to them. Even the mighty Sikorsky helicopter would have a difficult time slicing through this storm, which Newton was certain was a five (at last, a fucking five!). For another, there wasn't a lot of time, as in no time at all: the lady was a goner. But Jimmy wasn't about to argue with Maywell Hope, and besides, you can't be a useless shit *all* your life. So Jimmy Newton crawled away to find the portable generator.

Lester had been delivered onto the land. God had answered his prayer, even though it had been petulant ("Are You going to help out or what?"), and because he had been granted salvation, he knew there was some task he was meant to accomplish, a greater good to serve. Lester understood that the electricity was gone—it was gone on the entire island, the stars that indicated civilization had flickered and died—so he approached the shack that housed the generator. The little building was withstanding the tempest admirably. He grinned with satisfaction, because he'd built the thing. He was aware that his skills as a handyman were subpar, certainly not on a level with his skills as gardener, but he'd built the little shed and apparently done it well.

He was going to start the generator, head back to the main building and then plead with Polly to give him more liquor. The Lord made liquor, after all, for just such an occasion. Lester felt the one-hundred-and-fifty-*third* sam coming to him; he'd been waiting for many, many years, and now it was coming and it began, *Oh, Lord, Thou hast taken Thy grain and rendered it into golden water . . .*

He was about ten feet away from the shack when the wind spun him around like a top. Lester was dancing with a wind devil, an uncouth bully boy. He found that it was best not to battle, so he closed his eyes, opening them only when he sensed release; and when he opened them, he could see, dimly, that he was being torpedoed toward the generator shack.

When his head met the wood, the shed blew apart. It seemed no more substantial than if Lester had constructed the thing out of Popsicle sticks. He landed on top of the generator, a metal box that sat like a squat god upon a slab of concrete. His own wind was knocked from him, rushing away to join in the great celebration. He clung to the generator and tried to breathe, and while he was doing so, he tried to recall how to start the thing. He had to flip one lever down, another up, but this had to be done correctly. If he confused down with up, up with down, then the machine would create no power, it would only sputter and die, and then Maywell would be cross with him. Maywell would whip the hat from his head and wipe his brow with the back of a hand and mutter, "Lester, how many damn times do we have to go over this?" Lester would be forced to grin and shrug like an idiot. "Sorry, sir," he would say. And although he hated calling Maywell "sir," he wished he was having that conversation right now.

The levers were on either side of the generator, and Lester remembered there was a phrase, some aid to memory that Maywell had invented. It went "Left down, up right." Lester was pretty confident that was the phrase, because he remembered that the second half made a word: *upright*. He grabbed for the levers and was about to move them when it occurred to him that *downright* was a word as well. His hands went back to the side of the machine, and he clung with all his might.

The storm wanted Lester and it wanted the generator too. Even though it was secured into the concrete with six-inch bolts, the whole machine rocked and bucked.

Downright upright. Lester knew that any power and light he created would be short-lived, but that was no reason to abandon the notion. Something hit him on the side of the head, but he was so intent that he hardly noticed. *Upright downright.* Lester decided to proceed along these lines: *down-right* was a bad word, at least it was so in Lester's experience. *Lester,* people would say, *you're downright lazy. Lester, you're downright drunk. Upright,* though, was a good thing. Men walked upright and were therefore better than monkeys. With that observation, Lester placed his hands on the levers and took a deep breath.

Maywell wanted to tell Polly of his imperfect love, but he worried that it would alarm her. If he were to do it now, she would understand that the situation was very grim. He was unwilling to admit to himself how grim the situation was, so he kept his silence.

Everyone kept his, her, silence. When Gail and Sorvig returned with the first aid box, they opened it and neither said aloud how useless the thing was, full to brimming with unguents for sunburn and a collection of Band-Aids.

Gail fingered through the contents and found the largest plastic bandage, a square perhaps two inches long and wide. Sorvig plucked out a long ribbon of gauze. Sorvig said something to Gail, something that Maywell couldn't hear for the awful baying of the storm. "Just hurry up," he snapped, angry with the girls for possessing this dispassionate bedside manner, although he himself seemed poker-faced, detached.

Gail deftly tore away the outer wrap, removed the protective backing, which disappeared instantly. "Move your hand," she told Maywell. He lifted his fingers, and Gail capped the bloody well with the bandage. Then she lifted Polly's head slightly from Maywell's lap, and Sorvig began to wrap the gauze around Polly's neck.

Maywell told himself that Polly knew how he felt about her, despite the fact that his gestures of affection were rather crude; he was given to butt-slapping, for example. It was not as though Polly had ever told Maywell she loved him, either. He understood that in some sense she wasn't allowed to love him, not fully, because of the ghost of her dead husband. He often felt the ghost's eyes upon his back as he attended to his labours in the bedroom, and he sensed there was something, somewhere, that Polly was not offering to him. That had always been fine with him.

"Not too tight, now." He nodded toward the wrapping of the gauze.

Gail said, "Right," even though it was the other, Sorvig, who was undertaking the operation.

Mind you, the matter here was not whether or not Polly loved Maywell. That matter was gone—it had been plucked up by the tempest and blown out to sea.

"May," Polly said, although she had energy enough only to pop her pale lips apart, allow a little air to escape, shaping it into this sound that somehow made his name.

———

Jimmy Newton moved on hands and knees over broken glass, shards that shifted and swirled like the bottom of the sea. He thought about climbing to his feet, but the storm, trapped inside the dining room, was fierce and gladitorial, and Jimmy would simply be slammed up against the walls. Anyway, he had to locate the portable generator, and this lower vantage point would assist in that, so he tried to ignore the fresh cuts and lacerations he was acquiring with every second he spent on his knees and palms.

There wasn't a lot of dining room left, no longer much distinction between inside and out. Human construct and the distinctions it tried to impose upon the world didn't signify. It was like that game Jimmy played in airplanes, trying to determine when, precisely, the plane was entering a cloud. It was impossible; you could tell when the plane was outside the cloud, you could tell when the plane was inside, but there was no edge or border. The whole world was like that now, an endless moment of transition.

Jimmy Newton tried to remember where he'd left the portable generator, but the truth of the matter was that he didn't pay all that much attention to the details of his life. Never had, really. He'd never even *considered* paying attention to his life, that's how little attention he paid to it.

He crawled toward one corner of the room, but the contraption was not there. A chair rushed at him from out of the shadows, denting his forehead before lifting off slowly, awkwardly, like a helicopter with twisted blades. Jimmy Newton let out a little pained puff of air and a cuss word.

Then he was set upon by another inanimate object. This one was small, and scuttled through the opening made by his arms, nestling against his chest as though it wanted to suckle. Newton raised himself up on his haunches, took hold of the object, which was a box with two ports for video camera batteries. "Aha!" he exclaimed, and he cast a canny eye upwards. Jimmy had never thought much about heaven. The way he figured it, it was like the cloud game: he'd be able to tell if he was there, but he wouldn't be able to tell if he was entering.

CALDWELL HAD LEFT GALVESTON—he'd floated away with his family, the three of them clutching snapped timbers. Now he was back—he was back *now*—and Caldwell knew that time was running out, that the eye-wall was coming, that their world was going to be destroyed.

Caldwell gently spilled Beverly onto the bed. She reclined on one elbow, her back—and lovely backside—presented to him, through the dark and roiling mist. She raised her leg and he placed one hand on the bed and snugged the other between her legs so that his middle finger fell upon the moist lips of her pussy. His finger touched her clitoris, falling upon it with tentative authority. Beverly opened her legs wider.

The storm pushed him onto the bed, almost tenderly, as if Hurricane Claire wanted to get Caldwell out of the way while she destroyed what little there was left of cottage "K." Beverly reached down, took hold of Caldwell's cock, moved her wrist and hips slightly, and drew him into her.

She closed her eyes and listened. There was a sound that was louder than the wind now, though the wind was so loud that it caused a deep pain. The sound was the sea pounding upon Dampier Cay with redoubled insistence, a god come down from the heights to demand supplication and awe.

She was reminded of how the waves beat against the walls of her small home on Avenue C, the house she shared with

Margaret. The evening of September 8, 1900, the waves had come knocking and the water rose. Beverly mourned the ruination of the carpet on the floor below; she was sure that much of the furniture would need repair. But she was not worried, not terribly worried, until the first big crunching sound came.

"What was that again?"

Caldwell grunted, "Railway trestle."

"Right." Beverly took hold of the stained bedsheet and returned. There was another huge crunch. Margaret was terrified, then again, the girl was almost always terrified at some very profound level. This is why she valued so the touchstones of normalcy, because they gave the illusion that the world was not profoundly scarifying. This is why she insisted that her mother purchase Lowry's Cleansing Powder, because it was advertised widely and sold the most, even though Beverly knew there were other detergents that produced cleaner clothes. The crunching sounds kept coming, as though there were some monster out there with huge teeth and an endless appetite.

Beverly pressed down, eased up, trying to find the precise pressure that would bring release. Not that she was aware of doing this, because her thoughts were occupied with the huge crunches, the plangent thunderclaps.

The house began to shake, at first in coincidence with the trestle's assaults, and then independently of them and continuously. Beverly gathered Margaret into her arms. The child was too frightened to cry, although her little body spasmed with silent sobs. Beverly ran her fingers through Margaret's hair, long and golden and oh so soft because of the nightly ritual, two hundred strokes with the ebony hairbrush. Then she closed her eyes. She did not pray, because she was angry with God, but in her mind she bargained with Him, hard-nosed, almost belligerent, trying to negotiate safe delivery of her daughter.

No, said God.

"Yes," said Beverly.

She came as the timbers gave way, and screamed as the house collapsed and water rushed forward to claim her.

THE LIGHTS CAME ON just as Jimmy Newton crawled back into the Pirate's Lair with his portable generator. In the weak new light he saw the three people kneeling beside Polly. The girls were leaning back. There was nothing further they could do, this is what the attitude of their bodies told him. Maywell, on the other hand, was inclined forward, his head close to Polly's, waiting in case she had words to speak and breath left to speak them.

When the lights came on, Maywell looked around briefly and said, "Lester must have started the generator. Newton, get on the radio. Tell them we have an emergency."

Jimmy Newton abandoned the portable generator without rancour—even though he'd cut his hands and knees to ratshit getting the thing—lumbered to his feet and made for the bar, throwing himself through the opened hatch. The dial on the radio glowed very faintly. Newton took down the microphone, spun the dial to the emergency frequency.

"Miss Polly," called Lester from the passageway, "if you don't mind, ma'am, I would surely appreciate a drink." This was the sentence that Lester had composed and rehearsed—it was appropriately sober, both meek and assured—so his mouth spoke it even as his eyes tried to take in the scene before him.

Maywell looked up at him and said, "Damn you, Lester," and Lester was rocked on his feet, because Maywell had never damned him before, and Maywell's damnation possessed authority. Lester stumbled forward a few feet and then dropped to his knees. He tried to work out for himself what had happened, he tried to make sense of all the blood and the dark wrappings around Polly's neck.

Jimmy Newton was sending out an SOS. He knew the Mercator coordinates of Dampier's Cay, indeed that's how he knew his present location best, as numbers assigned to a particular conception of the world. So he spoke these into the microphone and chanted, "S-O-S." By way of response he received a lot of static.

"Tell them we have a medical emergency," Maywell Hope called out.

Newton didn't have the stomach, the *heart,* to tell Maywell that he was by no means confident the message was being received anywhere in the universe. So he said, "We need paramedics," into the microphone, adding, for Hope's benefit alone, "We have an injured woman here."

"I'm going to pray for Polly's soul," Lester told Maywell.

"She doesn't need you to pray for her soul," muttered Hope. Polly's lips were moving, but no words came.

Jimmy Newton couldn't resist. He spun the dial and found the right frequency and said, "NOAA? Come in, NOAA. This is Jimmy Newton."

"Newton?"

The voice was faint. Maybe it wasn't even there, but Jimmy was pretty confident he'd heard his own name. "What is she?" Newton demanded. "Is she a five?"

"Five," came the return.

Newton heard the word *five,* he was absolutely sure that NOAA had told him *five,* and Jimmy smiled and was about to rattle a fist in victory, but then Maywell appeared and delivered a right hand into Jimmy Newton's face. Newton crashed into the shelves that held the old radio. He covered his nose with his hands, because his nose was spurting blood in great quantities. Newton felt something hit his back, and he realized that the radio had tumbled from its resting place, so he spun around and tried to catch it. Newton managed to get his hands around it, but his hands were covered with blood and the housing was rendered out of some crude plastic that would have been hard to grab hold of under any circumstances. So he watched the radio fall to the ground, where it cracked open like an egg; he watched the light in the tubes flicker and die.

"Well," he offered, "we are now, like, totally fucked."

Lester was improvising a prayer, begging safe passage for Polly's immortal soul. He believed this to be his best prayer ever. He didn't really know what he was saying, but his heart was beating fast and strong, emotions were bubbling as though his insides were on the boil, so this had to be one motherfucker of a prayer. Lester loved Polly, too, in his way. He worked hard for her, harder than he worked for anybody else. And he found her beautiful, truly beautiful, one of God's finest womanly creations. She was so good and beautiful that her seat in glory was ensured; but Lester prayed hard anyway, as hard as he'd ever prayed, his best prayer ever.

Gail climbed to her feet and took a few steps. She poked her head forward and twisted her neck, taking a cautious look down the passageway, into the dining room. Wind rushed down to slap her face, but it did so with no great force, it was firm and tentative at the same time. She stepped forward and let the wind rush around her body, and although it forced her to take a step backwards, she reclaimed her ground. Things stirred in the dining room, stirred and twitched, like the extremities of a creature that was dying. "Hey," she called out, "know what?"

Lester finished his prayer. Polly's lips moved and Lester imagined that she said "thank you," but she was very far away now from the sad vale, and Lester didn't think, necessarily, that she was speaking to him. She could very well be addressing Our Lord, who was holding out His great hand and bidding her welcome. Lester imagined that Polly was gazing at Paradise, where there was gentle blue water and beautiful flowers, Birds of Paradise, Crowns of Thorns.

"What?" Sorvig was the only one listening.

"I think it's over."

Newton stepped through the hatch in the bar, wiping blood away from his face. "It's not over," he said.

Maywell Hope had the broken radio in his hands and was staring into its innards, hoping to see tubes flicker back into operation.

"Yeah, it is, I think," said Gail. "The sun's even coming out." At least, everything in the dining room was suffused with an odd violet glow.

"It's the eye," said Jimmy Newton. "The eye of the storm."

"How long did they say?" said Maywell, looking at Polly, afraid to go nearer, because his view was blocked by Lester, and she might simply be sleeping.

"I don't know if I got through," said Jimmy. "I don't think I did. Maybe. Even if I did, I don't know how long they'd be, they have to fly through the thing."

"But it's over," repeated Gail. She had seen nothing so odd as the lavender flush upon the new world, neither so odd nor so beautiful.

"It's not frigging over," said Newton. "We're in the eye of the storm. And we better get out of here."

"Where would we go?" whispered Sorvig. "To another building?"

"This is a five," said Newton, shaking his head.

"What do you mean, a five?" Maywell said.

"I'm talking the Saffir–Simpson scale, which is how they measure hurricanes. One through five."

"Numbers." Maywell spat the word with great disdain. "You know what, Jimmy? It is what it is."

"'Category five,'" recited Newton. "'Catastrophic. Winds greater than 155 miles per hour. Storm surge greater than eighteen feet. Complete building failures with small utility buildings blown over or away. All shrubs, trees and signs blown down. Major damage to all structures located less than fifteen feet above shore level and within five hundred yards of the shoreline.'" Newton took a pause. "That's us, baby."

Polly was almost gone now. Lester prayed for a miracle. The notion of miracles was the foundation of his idiosyncratic religion. When he preached, he featured all of the miracles mentioned in the Bible, and made up a few of his own—Jesus gesturing at the ground and causing flowers to burst upwards through the parched sand. It occurred to him that he might assist in the miracle (Lester was God's instrument, after all), so he bent forward and gave Polly the kiss of life. He locked his lips over hers and blew life into her body.

"So," said Sorvig, "let's get the hell out of here."

"But it's *over*," said Gail.

"It's not over, Gail," said Jimmy Newton. "We're in the eye. The other side's coming, and when it does, we'll be hit even worse."

Lester lifted his head and studied Polly's face. He thought he saw life flickering there, he thought that she was smiling now, happy to be returning, so he reapplied his lips.

"What the hell are you doing, Lester?" demanded Maywell.

Lester gestured at Miss Polly, demonstrating the reanimation he and the Lord were creating. But Polly lay very still.

Maywell began to move toward her, slowly.

"Where would we go?" asked Sorvig.

"There's only one place to go," answered Jimmy Newton. "*Up*. We go up the hill, get as high as we can."

"But there are no buildings there," argued Sorvig.

"I got bad news: there are no buildings *here*."

Maywell Hope pushed Lester aside and knelt down beside Polly. He placed his lips upon her own. Maywell didn't breathe hard, as Lester had done, Maywell kissed Polly as gently as he could. He had never done that, seen how lightly their lips could meet. He was not a man given to tenderness, and Polly had never minded. But now Maywell tried to be as gentle as he could, and he hoped that Polly would comprehend that his love, though imperfect, was the best thing about him. And during these moments Maywell hoped that she had life enough left to understand. And once he'd admitted in this way that his wife was dying, he had no choice but to admit to himself that she was dead.

BEVERLY CLIMBED OFF THE BED and looked around. She did this in a very leisurely manner, as though it were Saturday morning, reflected Caldwell, as though she were searching in the debris for the damned newspaper, which the boy tossed from his bicycle with frenzied insouciance. The wall that had existed between cottage "K" and cottage "J" had disappeared, and Beverly glanced through and saw not very much. The shower stall remained over there, tilted, a bed frame sticking out of its opening. A few uprights had survived the storm; the enamel washstand in "K" was still standing. It was a useless convenience, remembered Beverly, not hooked up to any piping, but there it was, full of warm water. "Hmmm," she said, turning back toward Caldwell and shrugging.

She was caught in a shaft of light that drove down from heaven with the determination of lightning and made her iridescent. Beverly's naked body shone different colours: her breasts were mauve and her stomach was kind of green, one leg was yellowish, the other pink. "You're beautiful," Caldwell told her, more informative than complimentary.

"Hey, look," said Beverly, and she pointed toward her feet. There were small pieces of light there, round and pulsating. These little balls of illumination moved about pell-mell, seeking sanctuary. "That's weird, huh?"

Caldwell climbed off the bed and went to join Beverly in the shaft of light. She smiled at him, stroked his chest. "We better get out of here," said Caldwell.

Beverly smiled, but in an odd way. "What do you mean?"

"Well," shrugged Caldwell, "this is the eye of the storm."

"Yes," agreed Beverly. "Soon the winds are going to come from the other direction."

"That's right."

"The winds are going to come from the other direction, and they will make everything right again."

"Ummm . . ."

"Things that the wind knocked over, it will make them erect once more. Things that it destroyed, it shall now make whole."

"No, Beverly."

She stretched upwards to kiss Caldwell's lips lightly. "You just wait and see," she whispered.

"The storm surge," said Caldwell, "is centred in the right side of a hurricane. You see, while the wind in the rear of the system is pushing toward shore, the wind in the front is pushing toward the centre. It's pushing toward the centre, piling up water against the rear. Do you understand?" Caldwell looked into Beverly's eyes, searching for enlightenment, just as he'd desperately searched the eyes of his students, hoping that they'd comprehended what he himself did not. But, Caldwell realized, he *did* understand, this time. In fact, he understood it all—the creation of the tropical depression, how it was set into motion by the Coriolis effect, the airy concept of organization. He realized that science wasn't a way to explain the world, science was rather a way in which the world *explained itself,* employing this shaky but shared vocabulary.

"I understand," said Beverly, her tone indicating that she understood without caring. "And this is compounded by the so-called *soda-straw effect.*"

"Exactly," said Mr. Caldwell enthusiastically. "When we suck on a straw, we cause a sudden decrease in the air pressure within the tube. That draws the liquid up. In the eye of the storm the pressure is the lowest, so the water around the wall rises, approximately one foot per every inch of barometric pressure." Caldwell spread his arms to demonstrate simplicity.

"So what?" demanded Beverly.

"So . . . we'd better get to higher ground."

"Why?"

"I thought I'd just explained all that."

Beverly went outside, that is, she stepped over a ghostly doorstep, and strolled down to the road, where the road used to be, kicking through dirty water. "Please don't feel that you have to stay with me," she called over her shoulder. "If you wish to get to higher ground . . ." Beverly looked to her left, where Lester's Hump loomed in the weak new light. But her interest was caught by something. "Hey. Look at that."

The little blue church still stood. It was soaking wet, and a couple of huge Afzelius fig leaves lay plastered on its rooftop. The gravestones, even the little wooden crosses, remained upright.

Caldwell came to stand beside her. She smiled at him, nodded in the direction of the blue church, took his large hand into both of her small ones. "It's kind of a miracle."

"I suppose," he agreed. Caldwell could hear the storm coming again, not a roar so much as a rumble, a huge freight train. A freight train, but the engineer was drunk and sleeping it off, dreaming of true love but knowing none. "But what I'm saying is, the surge is going to clear the cliff over there . . ."

"Go, then." Beverly pointed toward the summit of Lester's Hump.

"We'll both go."

"What are you thinking, Caldwell? That we are going to wed? That we are going to live happily ever after?"

Truthfully, Caldwell had got no further in his thinking than that they should try to escape. Beverly, on the other hand, had been thinking deeply. She'd thought about the life she'd abandoned in Orillia, Ontario, and wondered if there was any part of it that required her return. She didn't have to go watch her grandfather die, because it would be anticlimactic. The old man had perished years ago and was existing in an alcoholic half-life. She wasn't needed at the office; the papers she'd misfiled would turn up sooner or later. She had no friends, not a single one, and even the very odd clique of which she was a member—weather tourists, weather weenies—didn't accept her. They couldn't comprehend her relationship to cyclonic action, and they were sanctimonious regarding her employment of her physical self. All she had in her life, now, were memories of Galveston, 1900, and a phys. ed. teacher named Mr. Caldwell. And she had him forever; it would make no significant difference if the man wanted to seek salvation upon the hilltop.

"Go on," she told him. "I'll be fine."

"But the storm surge—"

"I understand about the storm surge."

"What will you do?"

Of course, it hadn't occurred to Beverly to do anything at all, but she gave an answer anyway, mostly because Caldwell seemed to need one. "The church," she said. "I'll go inside the church."

There was irony there, which pleased Beverly, even a kind of satisfying sarcasm, because Beverly knew she was damned. She had been born in the land of the damned, into a damned family, and had been damned all of her years.

Caldwell was damned too, because he'd allowed separation. He'd parted from his love. Caldwell had thought it was only for a short while, an hour or so, while they went one place and he remained in another, but now he realized that separation is an absolute, there are no qualifiers. You are either with someone or you are not.

"Okay," said Caldwell, and he began to walk toward the pale blue structure. "We'll take our chances in the church."

There had been no clear demarcation between being and non-being. It was like the cloud game, the heaven game. Polly slipped out of life, into death, and no one could say when, exactly, it happened. But they all knew when she was gone.

Maywell stood up and rubbed at his eyes, but he was always rubbing at his eyes and there was no evidence that he was now digging out tears. Gail and Sorvig reached out toward him, but their fingers made no contact. Jimmy Newton scowled, looked around and considered practicalities. Should he try to fix the radio, endeavour to rescind the SOS? He thought about that, even though he knew it was stupid shit, designed merely to take his mind off the woman with the waxy skin. The only real acknowledgment of Polly's death was a negative one: Lester fell silent. He'd had every faith that his prayers would not fail, and when they did, he was a bit stupefied.

Maywell went behind the bar. He bent over and lifted the hatch to the storage area, the crawl space, full of bottles, cases of soda and beer. Maywell jumped down through the opening, bent over and began to reorganize the beverages systematically. After all, a mess would irritate Polly, and he didn't want that. As soon as that thought raced through his mind, a tiny, unwanted souvenir from life, Maywell became angry, kicking at the cases, levelling them until they became a crude funereal dais. He hoisted himself out and pulled open a drawer, fishing around inside.

"We don't got oodles of time," said Jimmy Newton.

"Fuck you, Jimmy Newton," replied Maywell.

"Got you." Newton smiled at the others, shrugged, as though Maywell were his errant and idiotic brother.

"Are you sure the storm's not over?" asked Gail. There was light, after all, bolts of colour that broke through the clouds. Dawn was approaching, so things felt like they were getting back to normal, the wheel once more spinning truly.

"It's not over," said Sorvig with finality.

Lester considered saying, "What will be, will be," but then decided, in a trice, that he was done saying it forever. Some things could be otherwise, in another vale or Holy

Realm. Lester hadn't reasoned it all out, but he would before his next sermon, and this notion would form his text. He wondered which islanders would be around to hear it, he even wondered where he might deliver it, because Dampier Cay would not be the same. The work of ages had been undone in a few short hours.

Maywell Hope found a piece of paper and a pencil, and scrawled out a few words. He bent over Polly's body and arranged it somewhat, smoothing her hair behind her ears, folding her hands across her chest, pressing this piece of paper between her cold fingers. Then he lowered his lover's body into the storage area. He stood up and slapped his hands together, which he knew looked, at best, odd, but he was not trying to rid his hands of death, he was trying to approximate as best he could a proper interment, and this is what he might have done had he thrown a handful of dirt upon sweet Polly to wish her a safe journey. He had been born with a black mark beside his name, but Polly had never noticed. Maywell was going to miss her very much.

"Lester," he said, "maybe you'd say a few words."

"Lord," said Lester, "this is Polly."

Those words had come to Lester easily enough, but once he'd spoken them, he felt the oppression of silence.

"Polly," he said after a few long moments, "this is our Lord."

Maywell threw the trap door shut. "We need rope. Come along, Lester."

Maywell headed toward the check-in desk, and Lester trotted eagerly to catch up. "I know where there's rope, Maywell. There's some underneath the counter."

Maywell stopped abruptly, turned back, and Lester's first thought was that he had angered him. Maywell reached out and clamped his hand on Lester's shoulder, tightening his grip so much that Lester felt pain and had to let out a small moan. "Lester," said Maywell, "we need to save the guests."

Lester nodded.

"I'm counting on you to help me. Now, you won't let me down."

"I won't let you down, sir."

"Don't call me *sir*, Lester."

"I won't let you down, Maywell."

Maywell nodded. "Lester, guess what? I've given up smoking."

"Yeah?"

"Leastwise," said Maywell Hope, "I don't expect I'll have another cigarette before I die."

The two men laughed, and for a moment were once again both Merry Boys.

THE FIVE PEOPLE CAME OUT OF THE MAIN BUILDING. They were bound together with rope, lengths of six feet or so connecting them at the waist. They were tied together in two separate groups. Lester was tied with Gail on one side, Sorvig on the other; Maywell and Jimmy Newton were bound.

"Now where's the other two?" asked Maywell.

Jimmy Newton said, "If anyone can look after himself, it's Caldwell. And he'll take care of, um . . ."

"Beverly," supplied Maywell.

"Yeah." Jimmy realized that he understood something, without really understanding it at all. "Look, they're fine. They're all right. We should get to where we're going. There's not much time."

They looked toward Lester's Hump, a huge black shadow hundreds of yards away.

"Let's go," said Maywell.

The quickest way to the summit of Lester's Hump was to follow the crest formed by the cliffside. It was safer, perhaps, to descend to the road, to follow it up the rise, but it would add minutes to the journey and they all could see that minutes might be precious. A huge wall of black rose to the east. It fell as evenly as a curtain and dropped from the top of the sky. All of the elements were commingled there: water, of course, and wind, and fire (because lightning sparked, the forks meeting to form geometrical patterns), and earth (because the black wall contained land that had been destroyed along the way, pieces of islands that were now naked and barren). They took a moment to behold the sight, and each recognized it in his or her own way. Maywell Hope heard the voice of William Dampier: *The Sky looked very black in that quarter.* Gail saw something that she'd seen in a nightmare. Sorvig was taken back to her grandfather's knee. The old man, strangled by a clerical collar, his face florid and his beard bone white, would often tell his little granddaughter how the world would end, and it was in this very manner, both chaotic and strangely organized. Lester saw a colour plate from the family bible, though he didn't know what particular story or parable it illustrated, because Lester couldn't read. He had never expected to see this one made real by the Almighty.

Jimmy Newton saw what he'd always wanted to see, a category five coming to meet him.

They began to walk along the crest. The edge of the island lay twenty feet away. Even so, they would often be slapped by waves, the foamy debris of waves shattered upon rock.

To their left, down a scarp, sat the pale blue church. They all wondered how it had survived, everyone except Jimmy Newton, who had heard countless stories of such anomalies, how one man's house was destroyed but his neighbour's left standing. Anyway, thought Newton, the blue church didn't represent that much of a freaky occurrence, not in the long run, because it would be crushed by the storm surge. Newton cast a glance to his right, toward the storm, and added a few words to that reflection: *any minute now.*

Newton had time on his mind. He looked ahead and squinted. It was difficult to see anything, both because the storm filled the air with dark wind and because day hadn't yet arrived. But it seemed to Newton that they didn't start to actually climb for a couple of hundred yards, which would take them maybe five minutes at the rate they were going. Then he looked again toward the black wall and judged the progress it had made. It was coming awfully fucking fast.

"Let's go, Newton!" shouted Maywell Hope, as though Jimmy had been dawdling, which is kind of funny, because Newton had only been *thinking* about dawdling. "To the left!"

"Yeah, yeah, yeah." Jimmy made a subtle change in direction, enough of one, he hoped, to satisfy Hope. He reached into one of his jacket pockets and began to fumble with the camera there, a little thirty-five-millimetre automatic. He slipped his hand through the strap, popped off the lens cover.

"Hurry up," said Maywell, and he spoke it in very even tones, which, for him, indicated great panic.

Jimmy Newton was tempted to glance to his right now, but that might give him away. Anyway, he could *feel* the eyewall. All of his other senses were tuned to it, gauging its advent. The bottom of Lester's Hump was approaching; they would soon begin to climb to its summit and a very slim chance of survival. Jimmy Newton imagined Oprah saying, "If I were you, all I would have been thinking about was getting up that hill!"

"Ah," Jimmy Newton would say, smiling a sly smile, something he would have to practise in front of a mirror, "you don't understand the way my mind works."

"I don't think any of us do," Oprah might say, which would get a big laugh.

But Maywell did. He understood the way Jimmy's mind worked. He couldn't comprehend the whys and the wherefores, but he did understand *how* Jimmy Newton behaved. The same as Maywell understood the comings and goings of bonefish.

So Maywell knew that Newton was bewitched by that thing to his right, the colossus that panted and slobbered and groaned and licked at them, judging their tastiness. Like all pirates, Maywell had a fear of drowning at sea; he'd never suspected that the sea was capable of coming after him, of snatching him away even though he stood on land. But indeed it was, and indeed it was coming, and when Newton turned toward it, Maywell was ready.

Jimmy rushed toward the edge of the island and drew the little camera up into position. His index finger found the shutter and he squinted into the viewer. All he could see was black; Newton glanced up to check his subject.

And he saw the wall of black towering over him.

Maywell Hope tackled Newton from behind, rolling into the back of his legs, causing Jimmy to buckle and fall to his knees. "You idiot," he snarled, "what the jesus fuck do you think you're doing?"

Jimmy Newton raised his camera as though it were an offering to the black god that loomed before them. "Getting the shot." These were the last words ever spoken by Jimmy Newton.

The wall of water hit Dampier Cay. It did not crash upon it, this was not a huge wave, you shouldn't think of it that way. This was a sudden translocation of the ocean itself. Some water was stopped by the land, but twenty-odd feet (NOAA later estimated the surge at a phenomenal forty-five feet) was simply sliced free by the sharp edge of the cliff. It drove across the island, looking to mate with other water. Water searches out water, that is a tenet of science so basic that even Caldwell understood it.

The water took with it everything that was not bedrock, including Maywell Hope and Jimmy Newton. Gail saw them disappear, at least was fairly certain that she did, although this certainty arose not so much from memory, rather from the force with which the image appeared to her as she slept, months later. She saw Maywell and Jimmy offering no resistance to the water, clutching each other like lovers.

She thought she saw them go by; Gail herself was stationary, because Lester and the girls had achieved the rise, made an ascent of a few feet, not enough to clear the water but enough that they weren't claimed by the inundation. The girls were slapped and buffeted, but they were battered against land, smacking into trees, into rocks. Sometimes Gail and Sorvig did find themselves floating away, but then they would feel pain in their waists, intense but reassuring, ropes carving into their skin. Gail and Sorvig were pulled back to earth.

And Lester held onto a rock, a rock that perhaps flowered from the very belly of the earth, because it was not moved by the storm. Lester held onto this rock for life, dear life. The rope around his waist was pulled so tightly that he had little air, little breath, but that was all right, because Lester had no prayers to offer.

LATER THAT SAME DAY came helicopters, some finally able to respond to Newton's SOS, the others dispatched by news organizations. The reporters were dressed in foul-weather gear, even though the storm was far away now, dissipating over Mexico. The reporters wore yellow and green rubber suits that covered them head to toe; the hoods had oversized brims, and these covered their faces and looked like bills, so it seemed as though a strange new species had descended upon what was left of Dampier Cay, a mutation that was half human, half fowl. The reporters scurried around, some of them photographing the debris, others speaking into little machines, recording their impressions.

The reporters found Polly's body in the storage area. There was a soggy note in her hand, held so tightly in her fingers that it tore when the reporters tried to remove it. They pieced the note back together and read, *This is Polly Greenwich. She is a good woman. I love her very much. Maywell Hope.*

The reporters chronicled the story in various ways. Some implied that Maywell simply threw the body into the storage area and then hightailed it; others managed to convey a sense of reverence and ritual, Maywell taking his time despite the danger to himself. None of the reporters got the story right, of course. None wrote that the Last of the Merry Boys was gone forever, that while Hope may have been born with a pirate's heart, he died with a finer one.

The reporters and rescue workers went up Lester's Hump, and at the very summit they found a black man and two white women. The three were sleeping, all with small smiles upon their lips, as though they were entertaining delightful dreams. The man wore overalls and a white shirt, and despite everything, his clothes had a sense of neatness about them. The girls were pretty and their clothes were tightened around their bodies by the heavy rains. Their photograph was on the front page of many newspapers. Gail Forster and Sorvig Laskin became known as the "Hurricane Party Girls," and although they initially distrusted the label, they soon learned that it conferred a certain amount of respect.

The reporters didn't think there was much of a story in the case of Jimmy Newton, and his name was only mentioned once or twice in the newspapers. Mind you, there was considerable buzz on the Internet, weather weenies posting tributes and reminiscences. They felt a keen sense of loss, not that anybody really liked Jimmy. But he was Mr. Weather, and without his guidance the others were left to their own hunches, their best educated guesses. The globe once again became daunting, unknowable, so they mourned Jimmy Newton and called him the best there ever was.

You might think it sacrilege that Beverly and Caldwell made love once again in the little church, the church that was painted the same shade of blue as a perfect sky. It is true that there was anger in Beverly's heart, that she took a mischievous satisfaction in falling to her knees in front of the wooden cross, folding her hands with mock piety and then collapsing forward.

Caldwell knelt behind her and guided himself inside. Beverly began to hum and hoot and finally to shriek at the top of her voice. She shrieked so that God might hear her over the storm, so that He might understand her anger. But those of you who think this sacrilege must therefore believe that God knew all about Beverly's anger, and was forgiving. And you must believe that when the water crested the cliffside and began to gather up everything that lay in its way, you must believe that it picked up the church almost carefully, the entire pale blue structure, and carried it away to sea. You will temper your belief with what you know of science, and conjecture that this challenges credibility. All right, perhaps it does, but you might believe that when the pale blue church was destroyed, crushed by the huge hands of Hurricane Claire, some of the planks remained attached to the laths, and could serve as rafts. And you can imagine that Beverly and Mr. Caldwell rode these rafts upon the waves until they came to the shore of a small island where the natives, naked and smiling, greeted them with gifts.

The author of eight novels, PAUL QUARRINGTON is also a musician, an award-winning screenwriter, a filmmaker, a playwright and an acclaimed non-fiction writer. He won the Governor General's Literary Award for Fiction for *Whale Music* in 1989 and the Stephen Leacock Medal the year before for *King Leary*.

QUARRIN   Quarrington, Paul.
           Storm chasers.

$23.95

DATE			